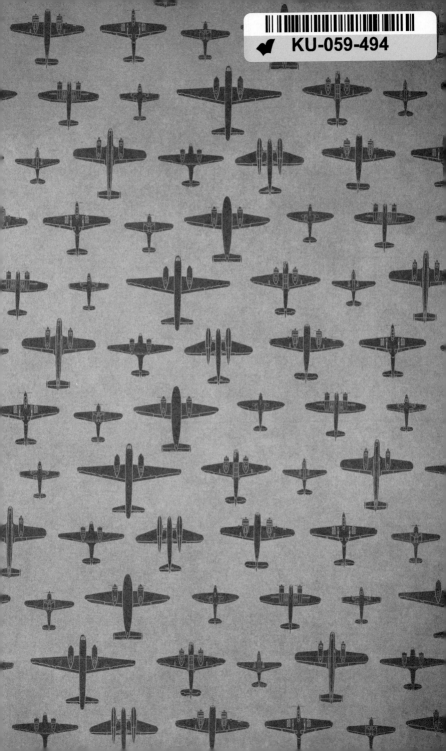

KU-059-494

Biggles in the Baltic

William Earl Johns was an English adventure writer, best known as the creator of the beloved Biggles stories, which drew on his experience as a pilot in the First World War. After his flying career with the RAF, Johns became a newspaper air correspondent, an occupation he combined with editing and illustrating books about flying. He wrote over 160 books, including nearly 100 Biggles titles.

Also by Captain W. E. Johns and published by Canelo

Biggles' WW2 Adventures

Biggles in the Baltic
Biggles Sees It Through
Biggles in Borneo

Biggles Between the Wars

Biggles Flies North
Biggles, Secret Agent
Biggles in the Jungle

Biggles, Special Air Detective

Sergeant Bigglesworth, CID
Biggles: The Second Case
Biggles on the Hunt
Biggles Takes a Holiday
Biggles Breaks the Silence

BIGGLES
in the
BALTIC

CAPT·W·E·JOHNS

CANELO

First published in the United Kingdom in 1940 by Oxford University Press

This edition published in the United Kingdom in 2022 by

Canelo
Unit 9, 5th Floor
Cargo Works, 1–2 Hatfields
London, SE1 9PG
United Kingdom

A CIP catalogue record for this book is available from the British Library.

Print ISBN 978 1 80436 060 6
Ebook ISBN 978 1 80032 910 2

Introduction © John Nichol 2022

The moral authority of John Nichol to be identified as the creator of the introduction has been asserted in accordance with the Copyright, Designs and Patents Act, 1988

Look for more great books at www.canelo.co

Printed and bound in Great Britain by Clays Ltd, Elcograf S.p.A.

1

Introduction

The Biggles books were some of the first I ever read, holding a special place in my heart, as they do for so many readers the world over.

I was transfixed by Biggles, Algy and Ginger's daring dogfights with the Germans in the World Wars, their secretive actions behind enemy lines under the nose of the nefarious Erich von Stalhein, and their adventures to far-flung corners of the globe in search of lost gold or missing friends. And, no matter where Biggles & Co. went, they took with them an unfailing and irrepressible sense of adventure, heroism and the calm certainty that they were fighting for something bigger than themselves, often with an almost casual disregard for the danger they were putting themselves in.

Captain William Earl Johns and I share a professional association: he as a pilot in the Royal Flying Corps in WWI, me as a Tornado navigator in the Royal Air Force. While propellers had been replaced by jet engines when I took to the skies, the freedom of flight, of being up there above the clouds, is something that all aviators know and love. And it is this freedom that typifies so many of Biggles's adventures when airborne travel, navigation and reconnaissance were a relatively new concept.

The stories span the globe, letting readers imagine faraway lands and the dangers they held from the safety of their favourite reading spot. In response to some summons or crisis, Biggles would often hop into his aircraft and fly to Belize, Borneo, or northern Canada, completing journeys in hours that would have taken days or weeks by other means, tackling problems – and villains – in this new frontier: the sky.

That imagination was further fired by Johns's passionate descriptions of the aircraft themselves. Whether it was a Sopwith Camel, the trusty Spitfire, a Bristol Blenheim or a Beaufighter, to read Biggles was to get caught up in the characters's love of flying machines. It is still possible to see some of those early aircraft at airshows today, where the famous drone of their engines provides a glorious soundtrack that echoes from the pages of these stories.

But why do the stories still hold such a strong appeal for readers, both new and returning?

For me, it is because the Biggles stories hark back to a simpler time now lost to us, before telecommunications, social media and the internet dominated our lives, when aerial combat was a duel of skill and chance in the skies. Biggles's aircraft didn't bristle with the mind-boggling array of electronic countermeasures, radar and laser-guided munitions of the Tornados I flew. For him, it was just his engine, and the stick and pedals that controlled the machine in a beautiful mechanical symbiosis.

It is also Biggles's courage and ability to improvise in the face of adversity – not to mention the bravery of his team, whom he had to trust with his life – that keeps readers coming back. Biggles, Algy and Ginger conducted daring adventures with a sense of decency, positivity and honour, and expected the same code of ethics from their allies and enemies alike, as can be seen in their numerous run-ins with von Stalhein!

Combine this unfettered passion and these incredible characters with Johns's seemingly inexhaustible supply of adventures (he wrote almost 100 Biggles tales), and you have a perfect recipe for a series that pulls the reader back, and leaves a lasting impression of the hero. Perhaps a hero we would all like to see in ourselves?

These new hardback editions from Canelo capture the essence of the Biggles books, with wonderful new covers featuring the very aircraft that appear in the novel in operation. They are also editions to be treasured, easily taking pride of place on the shelf of any Biggles fan, old or new.

I wish you many happy hours reading them.

John Nichol
Sunday Times bestselling author of *Spitfire*, *Lancaster* and
Tornado
www.johnnichol.com
Hertfordshire, March 2022

Biggles in the Baltic

CHAPTER I

The Call to Arms

As the momentous words 'England is now, therefore, in a state of war with Germany' came sombrely over the radio, Major James Bigglesworth, D.S.O., better known as Biggles, switched off the instrument and turned to face his friends, Captain the Honourable Algernon Lacey, M.C., and 'Ginger' Hebblethwaite. There was a peculiar smile on his face.

'Well, that's that. It looks as if we are in for another spot of war flying,' he murmured with an affected unconcern which did not deceive the others, who realised full well the gravity of the situation.

'Seems sort of unreal, as if something which you thought had only been a dream had suddenly come true,' remarked Algy quietly. 'What are we going to do about it?'

Biggles shrugged his shoulders. 'For the moment – nothing,' he answered. 'This isn't the time to go worrying the Air Ministry. They know all about us; no doubt they'll send for us as soon as they're ready. As far as we personally are concerned, we have this consolation: we do at least know something about the job – I mean, war flying – and that gives us an advantage over those who don't. We had better stand by in case the Air Ministry tries to get into touch with us. I only hope they'll let us stick together and not send us to different squadrons. I—' He broke off as the telephone bell shrilled. 'Hello, yes,' he went on, answering the call. 'Yes, Bigglesworth speaking – right you are, sir, we'll come right along.' He replaced the receiver. 'I'll give you one guess who that was,' he said drily.

'Colonel Raymond,' suggested Algy softly.

'Quite right. He's already back at his old job on Air Intelligence. He wants us to go along and see him at the Air Ministry right away. Call a taxi, Ginger.'

-

'Bringing us here doesn't sound as if we're going to an ordinary service squadron,' remarked Algy suspiciously, as they entered the Air Ministry and took the lift.

'We shall soon know,' returned Biggles briefly, as he knocked on the Colonel's door.

Colonel Raymond gave them a smile of welcome as he rose from his desk and came to meet them. 'Glad to see you all looking so well,' he said cheerfully. 'I've got a job which I fancy should suit you down to the ground.'

'Not *too* suicidal I hope, sir,' grinned Biggles.

The Colonel indicated three chairs. 'I wouldn't call it suicidal, although I'm not going to pretend that it's likely to be all plain sailing. If it was I shouldn't waste *you* on it, you may be sure. At a time like this we need our best men for special jobs.'

'Nice of you to put it that way, sir,' acknowledged Biggles.

'I presume that you are willing to come back into the service?' inquired the Colonel.

'What about Gin – I mean Hebblethwaite? He hasn't been in the regular service yet.'

'If you take on the job I'll see that he is gazetted as a pilot officer right away.'

'Good,' nodded Biggles. 'What's the job, sir?'

Colonel Raymond pointed to a map of Europe that nearly covered one wall of his office; its varnished surface was decorated with drawing-pins of different colours, each marking a point of strategical importance. 'I need hardly say that what I am going to tell you must be treated in strictest confidence,' he said earnestly. 'One careless word might undo the work of months. Incidentally, Bigglesworth, I may as well tell you that you were earmarked for this particular job months ago; in fact, it would hardly be an exaggeration to say that the job was specially created for you. What I mean is, had we not known someone capable of handling it we should hardly have dared to formulate such a dangerous plan.'

The Colonel picked up a long ruler and indicated on the map the area of ocean separating northern Germany from Scandinavia. 'Here is the Baltic Sea,' he continued, tracing the coastlines of Germany and East Prussia. 'You will readily perceive that anyone operating in these waters would be within easy striking distance of enemy country.'

A puzzled look came over Biggles's face. 'But the Baltic is Germany's own sea—' he began.

Colonel Raymond held up his hand. 'Not entirely,' he argued. 'Germany does, more or less, control the Baltic, but other countries have an interest in it – Lithuania, Latvia, Finland, Estonia, and the Scandinavian countries. You may say, naturally, that they are all neutral. Quite right, they are, and it would be a serious matter if the neutrality of these countries were violated, either intentionally or accidentally. I am now going to let you into a secret so vital that its importance could hardly be

3

exaggerated. Some time ago, perceiving that war might not be averted, we took the precaution of acquiring from one of the countries I have named an uninhabited island so small as to be negligible. Its name is Bergen Ait. It is in fact no more than a mass of rock, quite useless for any commercial purpose. Nevertheless, it embodies a feature that made it worth the large sum of money we paid for it, although here I should say that no one outside the countries concerned is aware of the transaction – that the island is British property, entitling us to use it as a base. It is remote, and in normal times I don't suppose anyone lands on it year in year out. Naturally, being so small, it could not easily be defended against enemy forces, so its only value to us lies in its secret character. The special feature to which I referred just now is a cave that has been worn into the very heart of the rock by the action of the waves. This cave is large enough to house several aircraft. You will now begin to see what I am driving at.'

'I understand,' replied Biggles quietly. 'The idea is to establish a base right on the enemy's doorstep, so to speak?'

'Precisely. From this base raids will be launched on military objectives, some of which have already been decided on, places which could not very well be reached from England or France. We have been preparing this depot for some time. The aircraft are, in fact, already there, as well as other equipment likely to be required, all ready for "Z" Squadron – as we have decided to call it – to take over. I need not describe the equipment in detail now, but in case you wonder – if you go – what the skis are for, I must tell you that in winter the sea is often icebound, and the squadron will be frozen in. For the rest we shall have to rely on the Commanding Officer to use his initiative in dealing with the difficulties and dangers that will certainly arise – events that are impossible to foresee.'

'How is this officer going to get there, since the Baltic is, anyway, at this moment, controlled by the German fleet?'

'There is only one way – by submarine,' replied the Colonel calmly. 'The submarine will land the party there – and leave them there.'

'I see.'

'You understand that the job is essentially one for volunteers; you needn't take it on if—'

'I don't think we need discuss that, sir,' interrupted Biggles.

'Good. I knew you wouldn't let us down. Make a list of the personnel you think you will be likely to require and I will arrange with the Admiralty for underwater transport. Don't take more men than is absolutely essential. The fewer there are the longer the stores will last.'

'One question, sir. I imagine the base is equipped with radio?'

'It is.'

'That means we shall get orders from time to time?'

'Yes.'

'Are we to confine ourselves to these operations, or am I at liberty to take action on my own account – always assuming that such action is, in my opinion, worth the risk involved?'

Colonel Raymond was silent for a moment or two. 'That's a difficult question to answer,' he said slowly. 'Naturally we are anxious to preserve the secret of the base as long as possible, but if I said "no" to your question it might mean losing a chance to strike a vital blow at the enemy. I shall have to leave it to your judgement.

But if you do take on anything on your own account the responsibility will be yours.'

'That's fair enough, sir,' agreed Biggles. 'Are there any special instructions?'

'There are, but I can't give you them now. You'll sail under sealed orders, and receive instructions concerning them by radio when you have established yourself at your base. When is the earliest you can start?'

'Now, sir.'

Colonel Raymond smiled. 'That's a bit too early for me. Today is Sunday; I will arrange for you to embark on Wednesday morning. We'll have another chat before then; there are one or two minor points I shall have to discuss with you. There is one thing…'

Biggles waited.

'Frankly, I think it is certain that sooner or later the enemy will discover your hiding-place,' continued the Colonel, his eyes on Biggles's face. 'You may last three months – a month – or only a week; it depends upon how things fall out. We must do the best we can with the time at our disposal. As far as we know, the German Intelligence Service has no suspicion of what is afoot, but one can never be quite sure. Bergen Ait is no great distance from Kiel, where an old acquaintance of yours is in charge.'

Biggles raised his eyebrows. 'An old acquaintance? You don't by any chance mean—'

'Von Stalhein. Erich von Stalhein – no less. He was bound to be given an important command.'

Biggles smiled faintly. 'Von Stalhein, eh?' he murmured reflectively. 'You know, I've almost got to like him. He hasn't had the best of luck in his encounters with us—'

'It is to be hoped, for your sakes, that he doesn't have the best of luck this time,' said Colonel Raymond seriously. 'He has old scores to wipe out, remember. He's your worst enemy, and an implacable one. If ever he catches you—'

'We shall have to see to it that he doesn't,' put in Biggles lightly.

'That's the spirit,' agreed the Colonel. 'Well, that's all for the time being. I'll let the Air Chief Marshal know you're going. You ought to be able to do the enemy an immense amount of mischief before he finds you out.' The Colonel held out his hand. 'Good luck.'

'We shall do our best, sir,' promised Biggles.

CHAPTER II

'Z' Squadron Takes Over

Precisely a week later, a little after sunrise, the small party that comprised 'Z' Squadron, R.A.F., stood on a shelf of rock in the sombre heart of Bergen Ait, and watched the submarine that had brought them there creep like a monster of the deep towards the entrance to the vast cavern which the action of the waves had eaten into the islet. From the conning-tower, still open, projected the head and shoulders of the commander, his eyes on those he was leaving behind. He raised his hand in salute. 'Good hunting, boys,' he called. The words echoed eerily round the walls.

Biggles returned the salute. 'Good hunting yourself, sailor,' he replied.

That was all. The naval officer disappeared. The steel cap of the conning-tower sank into its bed; deeper and deeper into the water bored the long grey body of the underwater craft. Presently only the conning-tower could be seen, and as the vessel felt its way into the cove that sheltered the mouth of the cave, this, too, disappeared, leaving the airmen alone in their sinister war station.

Biggles turned and considered the members of his squadron. They were five all told, Algy and Ginger being the only pilots besides himself. Colonel Raymond had pressed him to take more, but Biggles felt that an outsider might upset the unity of a team which, from long and often perilous experience, had proved its efficiency, a team which had been forged in the fire of loyal comradeship. An extra member who was not in entire sympathy with them might easily do more harm than good, he reasoned, perhaps wisely.

In addition to the three pilots there was Flight-Sergeant Smyth, Biggles's old war-time fitter and rigger, whose skill with either wood or metal was almost uncanny, and who could be relied upon to work a twenty-four-hour day without complaint should circumstances demand it. With him was his son Roy, a lad of eighteen who had entered the Royal Air Force as a boy apprentice and had passed out as a wireless operator mechanic. Keen, alert, and intelligent, he promised to follow the footsteps of his father up the ladder of promotion.

The only other member of the squadron was an old naval pensioner appropriately named William Salt, already known to them as 'Briny', a nickname which he had carried for nearly half a century in the Navy. Nobody knew just how old Briny was, but he was apt to boast that he had started life as a boy in the days of sail, when steamers were few and far between. Biggles had applied to Colonel Raymond for a cook, feeling that one was necessary to save the others wasting valuable time in the kitchen. Briny had been, in fact, the cook on Colonel Raymond's private yacht (owing to the war the yacht had, of course, been laid up). Briny had put his name down for service and Colonel Raymond had recommended him confidently, despite his age, saying that he possessed a store of practical knowledge, apart from cooking, that would be useful to them. His only failing was (he warned them) a weakness for 'reminiscencing', but this was balanced by a shrewd cockney wit that might amuse them on their dreary station. So Briny had, to use his own expression, 'pulled up 'is mudhook' and come along.

'Well, here we are,' announced Biggles. 'There's little I can tell you that you don't already know. It may be rather alarming to be stationed in what are practically enemy waters, but no doubt we shall get used to it. We have this satisfaction: instead of being a mere cog in a vast machine, we are, as it were, a detached unit fighting a little war of our own, the success of which will largely depend on ourselves. I'm not going to make a speech, but there is one point I must mention. On a job like this, where everyone is in close contact with everybody else, ordinary service discipline is bound to be relaxed. This calling people by nicknames, for instance – as far as I, as commanding officer, am concerned, this may continue except when a person is actually on duty; or, since we shall all be on duty all the time, perhaps I had better say engaged on specific duty under my direct orders. Cooped up as we are, each is too dependent on the others to bother about ceremony, but I don't think familiarity need interfere with the efficiency of the unit. I know you'll all do your best. In the event of casualties, the next in order of seniority will, of course, take over. That's all. Roy, take over the radio room and stand by for reception of signals. Briny, you'd better get the galley functioning. The rest come with me; we had better make ourselves familiar with the layout of the depot before we do anything else.'

The servicing of the base at Bergen Ait had been carried out by the Admiralty, who, as usual, had done their job thoroughly. The islet itself was, as Colonel Raymond had said, merely a mass of rock rising to several hundred feet above the sea, the nearest land being the enemy coast of East Prussia. Less than a mile in circumference, for the most part the cliffs were precipitous, sterile, the home of innumerable sea-birds. Here and there, however, erosion had caused the cliffs to crumble, so that they lay in terrifying landslides to the water's edge.

One such collapse had flung a mighty spit of rocks some distance into the sea, so that a small cape, perhaps two hundred yards in extent, was formed. This served as a breakwater and at the same time formed what was, in effect, a cove that could be used as a harbour, but only when the sea was reasonably calm. In bad weather, or when the wind was blowing directly into it, the cove (so the Admiralty had informed Biggles) became a seething cauldron, dangerous for any type of craft. Even in fair weather the tides raced into the cove with considerable force, and it was no doubt due to this that the rock had been undermined, forming the cave, which, being at an angle, could not be seen from the open sea. One glance had been sufficient to warn Biggles that should an aircraft be caught out in bad weather it would be utterly impossible for it to get back into the cave. Indeed, as he had surveyed the scene from the submarine, he suspected that the natural risks of operating from such a base were likely to be as dangerous as the enemy. On the other hand, these very hazards had their compensations, in that they were likely to keep enemy shipping at a distance.

Although the entrance of the cave was low – hardly large enough to admit an aircraft at high water – inside it was as lofty as a cathedral, and ran back, diminishing in size, for a considerable distance, although the farther extremity had not yet been explored. It was obvious that, except at one place, the walls of the cave had dropped sheer into the water, but an artificial shelf (promptly named the 'catwalk' by Briny) had been cut to enable those inside to reach the bay. This shelf also served as a quay for mooring the aircraft and a small motorboat.

At one spot, however, a flaw in the rock had left a more or less flat area, about half an acre in extent, and every inch of this space had been utilised for the erection of several low wooden buildings. On inspection these turned out to consist of a small but well-fitted workshop and armoury combined, a mess-room with sleeping quarters and a record office attached, and storehouse packed with food, mostly tinned, although there were sacks of potatoes, onions, and other vegetables. The radio room stood a little apart, and from this also was controlled the electrical equipment both for lighting and for running the lathe in the workshop. A small oil engine, dynamo, and storage batteries were housed in a recess cut in the rock. Nearby was a rather alarming ammunition dump, long sleek torpedoes lying side by side with bombs of various sizes – high explosive, incendiary, and armour-piercing – as well as cases of small-arms ammunition. Another hut contained spare parts and medical and photographic stores.

'Well, I must say the Navy have made a thorough job of it,' observed Biggles with satisfaction, as the party concluded its tour of inspection. 'Let's go and have a look at the machines. Colonel Raymond told me that they were specially designed for the job. He could only let us have four – one each and one in reserve. Normally they will be used as single seaters, but there is a spare seat for a passenger, or gunner, with a gun mounting, under the fabric just aft of the pilot's seat. The spare seat can be made available by merely pulling a zip fastener. They're amphibians, of course; goodness knows where we shall have to land and take off before the job is finished. The outstanding feature, I understand, is a wide range of speed; what with flaps and slots we ought to be able to land on a sixpence. There are eight machine-guns, operated by a single button on the joystick. Incidentally, you'll notice that they are fitted for torpedo work, as well as with bomb-racks.'

'Well, it's a nice clean-looking kite, anyway,' remarked Algy as they stood on the ledge looking at the aircraft. 'By the way, what do they call them?'

'As far as I know they haven't been named,' returned Biggles. 'The official designation is S.I. Mark I.A. – the S standing for secret.'

'That's too much of a mouthful; we shall have to think of something shorter,' declared Ginger.

'Can you suggest anything?' inquired Biggles.

Ginger thought for a moment. 'What's something that sits in a hole and darts out at its prey?' he asked pensively.

'A rabbit,' suggested Algy.

Ginger snorted. 'I said *darts* out at its prey. Have you ever seen a rabbit dart at a dandelion?'

'What's something that whirls out, strikes, and then whirls back home again?' murmured Biggles.

'Boomerang,' answered Ginger promptly.

'Good,' cried Biggles. 'That sounds more like it. We're the Boomerang Squadron. It wouldn't be a bad idea if we gave each machine a name of its own, too, for identification purposes,' he added.

'In that case mine's *Dingo*,' announced Ginger. 'If we're the Boomerangs we ought to stick to Australian names.'

'An Aussie once told me that the dingo is a nasty, dirty, stinking little beast,' said Biggles, with a sidelong glance at Algy.

'He may be, but he's thundering hard to catch,' declared Ginger. 'I'm sticking to *Dingo*.'

'Then mine's going to be the *Didgeree-du*,' announced Algy.

'What!' cried Ginger incredulously. 'There ain't no such animal.'

'A fat lot you know about it,' grunted Algy. 'The didgeree-du is a bird.'

'As a matter of fact, the didgeree-du happens to be a native Australian musical instrument,' put in Biggles. 'It makes a lot of noise about nothing.'

'I don't care, I'm sticking to it,' insisted Algy doggedly. 'I like the sound of it.'

'Then I'll call mine the *Willie-Willie*', decided Biggles.

Ginger stared. 'You're not serious? What on earth is a willie-willie?'

'You'll know if you ever run into one,' replied Biggles grimly. 'I flew into one once, some years ago.'

'Flew into one? What are you talking about?'

'A willie-willie, my lad, is a cyclone, typhoon and hurricane rolled into one. It lurks round the north Australian coast and descends out of the blue in search of its prey, which it smashes, mangles, and finally blows to pieces. That's what I hope to do to the enemy.'

'Then *Willie-Willie* is a good name,' admitted Ginger. 'What about the spare machine? The duck-billed platypus is the only other Australian animal I know.'

'That's good enough,' agreed Biggles. 'But this won't do. We must get on. I'm expecting a signal through at any moment.'

They spent the next hour examining the machines, which, if appearance counted for anything, were capable of all that was claimed of them.

'What was that signal you were expecting?' inquired Ginger as they climbed out of the *Dingo* on to the catwalk and made their way towards the depot.

'That's something I can't tell you, the reason being that we're still under sealed orders. Admittedly they are in my pocket, but I can't open them until I get instructions.'

'I suppose the signal will come through in code?'

'Of course; all messages are in code in war-time,' answered Biggles. 'Well, there's nothing we can do except wait, so we may as well go along and see what Briny has produced for lunch.'

'What about trying out one of the machines?' suggested Ginger.

Biggles shook his head. 'No, for two reasons,' he decided. 'In the first place, it would be folly to show ourselves except when we are compelled to, and secondly, our petrol supply is not unlimited. As far as showing ourselves is concerned, I have an idea that most of our orders will be for night work, so we had better have a good look at the map.'

'It's going to be tricky work finding this lump of rock on a dark night, particularly if, as I presume, we shan't dare to show a light,' murmured Algy.

'It is,' agreed Biggles, 'but we shall have to do the best we can. It certainly wouldn't do to show lights except in dire emergency, because enemy ships might be close in to us without our knowing it, since in war-time ships don't carry lights, either.'

As they entered the mess Roy ran up with a slip of paper in his hand. 'Signal, sir,' he said, saluting briskly.

Biggles took the slip, glanced at it, and taking several envelopes from his pocket, selected one and ripped open the flap. For a minute or two he read in silence. Then, 'Listen to this,' he said. 'It concerns everyone. I'll read it aloud:

To Officer Commanding 'Z' Squadron. Standing routine orders.

1. These orders must be committed to memory by every officer in your command.

2. This document must on no account be taken into the air. It must not be allowed to fall into the hands of the enemy. In case of doubt it should be destroyed.

3. As they are at present planned, the duties of 'Z' Squadron will be confined to night operations, details of which will be issued.

4. Every precaution will be taken to prevent the enemy from becoming aware of the existence of the squadron, or its base. If an aircraft of the squadron is pursued by hostile aircraft the pilot concerned will not on any account return to his base, but will destroy his aircraft on the open sea.

5. Should the base be located by the enemy it must not be allowed to fall into his hands. All war material must be destroyed, no matter what sacrifice is involved.

6. Signals. Only in a case of utmost importance should radio equipment be used for

transmitting signals. Personal danger does not constitute a sufficient reason to transmit. If information of sufficient importance to warrant transmission is obtained, code will invariably be used.

7. Further supplies of food, fuel, and war material will be dispatched as the exigencies of the service permit, but it must be assumed that no such stores will be sent.

8. The greatest possible care will be taken not to violate the neutrality of non-belligerent countries.'

Biggles laid the paper on the table. 'That's all,' he said quietly. 'Quite enough to be going on with, too,' murmured Algy.

Briny appeared in the doorway. 'Lunch is ready, gen'l'men,' he said.

CHAPTER III

First Orders

By the following morning all the members of 'Z' Squadron were fairly settled in their new home and were becoming accustomed to the persistent lapping of the sea against the walls of the cave – a mournful, depressing sound that had disturbed Ginger's sleep. However, breakfast of ham and eggs, served by the ever cheerful Briny, soon dispelled the gloomy atmosphere.

'Have you got things sorted out in your department?' Biggles asked him.

'Ay, ay, sir,' answered Briny. 'This is a picnic to some of the places I've served. Why, I remember once in the Red Sea, chasing Arab dhows we was – let's see, it 'ud be about—'

'All right, never mind about that now,' interrupted Biggles.

'Ay, ay, sir!' Briny saluted and departed.

The airmen first went to the signals room, where they found Roy busy fixing up an alarum device that would rouse him should a signal come through while he was sleeping. Leaving him at his task, they made their way to the machines, on which the Flight-Sergeant was already working. Continuing along the catwalk, they reached the mouth of the cave and stood blinking in the daylight, notwithstanding that the sky was overcast.

Ginger climbed on a rock and surveyed his immediate surroundings. It was not a view calculated to induce high spirits. Under leaden clouds, a dark, choppy sea was beating sullenly at the foot of the cliffs, throwing showers of spray over the natural breakwater and nicking hungrily at festoons of black, slimy seaweed that lined the high-water mark. Above him, sea-birds of many sorts gathered on the numerous ledges or soared in the grey atmosphere like scraps of wind-blown paper. A movement a little farther along caught his eye, and he saw a seal drop into the water.

'Strictly speaking, we ought to mount a guard here,' opined Biggles. 'But if we did none of us would do any work or get any sleep.'

'I should go off my rocker, anyway, if I had to stand here and stare at this all day,' muttered Algy.

Biggles considered the heaving water speculatively. 'I should say that a vessel coming from that direction at night' – he pointed to the northeast – 'would see the reflection of our lights. I think it would be a good idea if we got some tarpaulins fixed up over the entrance to the cave.' He glanced up at the sheer face of the cliff. 'I don't think there's any question of exploring the island,' he continued. 'From what I can see of it, only an expert mountain goat could get to the top – not that I imagine there is anything there worth going up for. Well, there seems to be nothing more to see, so we may as well get back.'

On the way he gave the Flight-Sergeant orders about covering the entrance with tarpaulins.

Returning to the depot, they were in time to see Briny walking towards the galley with three fair-sized fish strung on a line.

'Where did you get those?' inquired Biggles.

'Out of the ditch, sir,' was the brisk answer. 'I thought that as 'ow we were living with the fishes, as you might say, sir, they ought to do their bit, so last night I dropped in a line or two to try me luck.'

'Smart work,' complimented Biggles.

'Why, lor' luv a duck, sir, that's nothing,' declared Briny, 'I've kept the whole ship's company going on fish before today.'

'*What!*' exclaimed Biggles incredulously.

Briny looked slightly embarrassed. 'Of course, they didn't get much each,' he admitted. 'But talking of fishin', I remember once, off Cape Horn, we got in amongst so many fish that they lifted the ship clean out of the water. I sez to Charlie, a shipmate o' mine, "Charlie," I sez—'

'Yes, all right Briny. Keep the story for a dull evening,' interrupted Biggles.

'Ay, ay, sir.' Briny touched the peak of his weather-soiled cap and went on towards the galley.

'I fancy he must sleep in that cap,' murmured Algy, 'I've never seen him without it.'

Further conversation on the subject was prevented by the arrival of Roy with a signal.

Biggles took the slip of paper. 'This, I fancy, is where we start the ball rolling,' he said, leading the way to the record office, where he unlocked a small safe and took out a red book carrying on the front, in large letters, the word SECRET. He sat down at the table to decode the message, and for several minutes was busy with pencil and paper.

'We do our first show tonight,' he said at last, looking up at the others. 'Zero hour is ten o'clock, weather permitting. Our objective is an ammunition dump on the south side of the Kiel canal, about three miles from the town. The dump can be identified by four long sheds standing close together, end on. The moon rises early, so we ought to have no difficulty in finding them.' Biggles filed the message and put the file in the safe.

'It sounds easy,' ventured Ginger.

'It may *sound* easy, but we may find it otherwise,' replied Biggles. 'In all Germany the worst hotbed of archie is at Kiel. Raymond warned me of that. After all, the Kiel Canal is probably the most important artery the Boche possess, so they've guarded it with their best anti-aircraft equipment. I think this is where we have to play the old soldier on them; if they hear us coming they'll knock us to pieces before we get anywhere near the dump.'

'And what is the "old soldier" in this case?' inquired Ginger.

'We'll climb to twenty thousand, cut our engines fifteen miles away and glide over. With luck they may not spot us until the first bomb bursts. Then the fireworks will start and things will probably get pretty warm. Ginger, you'll be new to this sort of thing, so I'll give you a tip. If you can't get high, keep low – the lower the better as long as you don't barge into anything. The lower you are the more difficult target you make for the gunners, since they can't swing their guns about like rifles.'

'Then we aren't all going over together?' put in Algy.

Biggles shook his head. 'It's too dangerous. We should probably collide in the dark. I think the best plan is to go over at intervals of ten minutes. I'll go first. As soon as I've unloaded my eggs the guns and searchlights will be after me; in the din they won't hear you coming, so you may get a chance to have an unmolested crack at the target. Algy, you'll follow me. Ginger, you'll be last, and if things pan out as I imagine you ought to get a clear shot. Take one bomb – a two-thirty pounder. If you lay it near the dump it ought to shake things up a bit. The instant you unload, shove your joystick forward and zigzag for the open sea. Then come straight home. To prevent us landing on top of each other in the dark I'll get Smyth to signal three flashes with a green light as an all-clear signal. He can stand by with the motorboat in case any of us makes a dud landing. That's all. We'd better get ready. Let's get the target marked on the map for a start.'

The rest of the day passed quickly, with all available hands preparing the machines for their perilous mission. They floated in line, in order of take-off, Biggles's machine leading, with two 112-pound high explosive bombs under the wings, and a nest of small incendiary bombs between the large twin floats. Algy's machine carried a similar load; Ginger's, the single 230-pounder, as Biggles had ordered.

As twilight fell the machines were towed nearer to the tarpaulins which the Flight-Sergeant and Briny had erected in accordance with Biggles's instructions. Biggles pulled one aside, and stepping into the open, surveyed the deserted sea reflectively; the sun, a ball of glowing crimson, was just sinking into the misty horizon. The wind had dropped and the sea was going down, as it so often does towards evening. He glanced at his watch. The time was eight-thirty. 'Everything seems to be all clear,' he remarked. 'Let's go and have a bite of food. By the time we've finished we shall be all set to give the gentle Hun a taste of his own medicine. I hope he likes it.'

CHAPTER IV

The Raid

At precisely ten o'clock, after a careful survey of the sea for ships, Biggles taxied out into the little cove under a moon that cut a swathe of silver light across the gently stirring ocean. The stars twinkled clear and bright in the autumn sky, into which the black silhouette of the rocky islet reared up like a mighty colossus. Without a glance behind him, he steered the *Willie-Willie* – its name now painted on the nose – into position for a clear run towards the open sea. The engine bellowed suddenly, and the machine surged forward, slashing a line of foam across the face of the water. The line ended abruptly as the aircraft soared like a gull into the air.

Holding the stick back with his knees, for the night air was as placid as a bowl of milk, he took a piece of chewing-gum from a pocket under the instrument-board and chewed it reflectively as he scanned the ever-widening horizon for lights; but neither gleam nor flash broke the sombre pall that war had laid over land and sea. Even the beacons of lighthouses and lightships had been extinguished. Only a weird blue glow illuminated the flickering instruments on the dashboard.

As the needle of the altimeter crept round the dial to the 10,000 mark Biggles turned the nose of his machine due south; still he climbed, but more slowly now as the air became more rarefied. Up and up – 12,000 – 14,000 – 16,000 – 18,000 – into a lonely indigo world; and still the machine bored upward. The blue light gleamed coldly on his face as he peered forward through the windscreen, looking for the land which he knew lay ahead. That Kiel would be 'blacked-out' after sunset was only to be expected, yet he thought there was a chance that the lights of moving traffic might reveal a road. But not a spark broke the stygian darkness.

At last the altimeter registered 20,000 feet, and the nose of the machine sank a little until it was on even keel; then, as the muffled roar of the engine died abruptly, the nose sank still lower and the *Willie-Willie* began to glide. The only sound was the soft hum of air passing over the surface of the machine.

Peering forwards and downwards, Biggles soon made out a vague mass which he knew was land, a vast black shadow that spread away until it was lost in the distance. Not a light showed anywhere. Turning to the right, he followed the coastline for a while, and then, after a glance at his compass and the moon, he headed straight towards it, losing height all the time, probing the darkness with his eyes, seeking the unmistakable landmark which he knew was there – the famous canal which connects the Baltic with the North Sea. At last he found it. The enemy might curtain their windows, but they could not curtain the moon, which, climbing higher, reflected itself on the water so that the canal lay like a silver ribbon across the sable land.

Biggles glanced at his altimeter again and saw that he was down to 8,000 feet; he would have wished to have been higher, for he still had some distance to go to reach his objective, but he dared not touch the throttle. One sound, and he knew that the silent atmosphere would be gashed by a score or more of blinding white searchlight beams. On he glided, the altimeter needle falling back as he followed the silver streak still far below.

He was down to 5,000 feet when at last he saw the slight curve in the canal that marked roughly the position of the ammunition dump. He could not see the actual buildings – he did not expect to – but he knew that they were there – assuming that Colonel Raymond's report had been correct, and this he had no reason to doubt.

He eased the joystick back until it was 'sloppy' in his hand, so near was he to stalling; but every mile gained now was of value, and although he hardly dared to hope that he would be allowed to get over the target without being detected, he intended to get as close as possible.

He was about a mile away when a searchlight beam thrust upward into the darkness like a steel dagger; for a moment it remained still, quivering, and then began a methodical quartering of the sky. Another joined it, and another, and he knew that the sound detectors had picked him up, in spite of the fact that his engine was only ticking over. He swerved away from the beams, and then put his nose down steeply towards the objective. In a moment a dozen beams were criss-crossing around him like gigantic scissors, as the operators below strove to get him in their grip. Suddenly one cut a colossal arc across the heavens; for a fleeting instant it flashed on his wings, and he knew that silence would no longer serve him. Almost viciously he thrust the throttle forward, and the engine bellowed its roar of defiance; simultaneously he pushed the nose of the machine down and sped like an arrow towards his target. In an instant the air was split by flashes, some, very close, bright orange; others, farther away, dull crimson, as the anti-aircraft gunners flung up a furious barrage. He did not alter his course, but held straight on in a screaming dive, leaving most of the flashes behind him.

His face, ghostly in the pale blue light of the instruments, was expressionless; his jaw was set, and his mouth a thin straight line. Something struck the machine with a thud that made it quiver. His lips closed a little tighter and his eyes flashed to the tell-tale instruments; but the set look on his face did not alter.

Not until he was down to 500 feet did he pull the machine out of its dive. Then, calmly and deliberately, as he brought it to even keel, he leaned over the side, seeking the sheds. Around him the air was torn and gashed by flame and hurtling metal, but he ignored it, as he knew only too well that to think about it was to court fear. So he concerned himself only with one thing – the sheds.

At last he saw them, stretching in a straight line along the edge of the canal, precisely as they had been described. He kicked out his right foot and dragged the stick in the same direction, sideslipping to bring the machine over them. Satisfied that he had gone far enough, he centralised the controls, keeping his eyes on the leading edge of the starboard plane at the place where it joined the fuselage, waiting for the sheds to appear. There was no question of using bomb-sights.

As the sheds came in line with the edge of the plane his hand closed over the bomb-toggle. An instant longer he waited. Then he jerked it back – one… two. The machine rocked as its load swung into space. Before it had properly recovered he had kicked out his right foot and was zigzagging at right angles from his original course; at the same time he held the joystick forward for all the speed he could raise, knowing that only speed could save him from the lines of white sparks that were streaming upwards, which he knew were tracer bullets.

He felt the explosion of the bombs rather than saw them, although the whole sky was lit up by a white glare; but the blast of air whirled the machine up like a feather caught in a gale of wind, and he braced his knees against the sides of the cockpit to steady himself. Banking vertically, he snatched a glance over his shoulder in time to see another explosion. The blaze half blinded him, but in the split second before it occurred he had noted that the end shed only was on fire. There was, he knew, a chance that the explosions caused by this fire would set the others off, for contrary to the general impression, an ammunition dump does not necessarily go up in one terrific explosion. It can catch fire and burn for a considerable period, sometimes weeks, with sporadic explosions from time to time.

With the anti-aircraft guns still pursuing him, he zoomed low again at the sheds, releasing his incendiary bombs in a shower; then, banking vertically, he raced towards the open sea. A searchlight picked him up and held him, nearly blinding him with its brilliant glare. For a moment or two he flung the machine about wildly, endeavouring to shake it off, but the beam clung to him like a leech. His nostrils quivered as a wave of anger surged through him. 'All right, if you want it you can have it,' he grated through his set teeth, and shielding his eyes with his left arm, he spun round and raced straight down the beam. His thumb found the button on the joystick and jammed it down savagely, and the machine shuddered like a frightened horse as eight streams of bullets poured down his path of flight. It was an old trick, and it worked. The light went out, either because it had been hit or because the operators had bolted for cover out of the withering hail. Satisfied, he swung the machine round on its original course towards the sea.

Most of the lights and archie flashes were now behind him, and he guessed the reason. The listening posts had heard the other machines. He glimpsed a fast-moving spark, like a firefly, held in a beam above him, and he knew that it must be Algy diving at the target. An instant later two terrific explosions in quick succession lit up the sky like a flash of summer lightning, and again the blast of air lifted the *Willie-Willie* bodily. There were no more explosions, from which Biggles gathered that Algy had missed the sheds, although an ever-spreading crimson glow suggested that he had set some buildings on fire, and since these must have had some connection with the dump the bombs had not been wasted.

The scene was now far behind him, too far for details to be picked out, so he allowed his nerves to relax and devoted his attention to the business of getting home.

Ginger, gliding at 5,000 feet towards the scene of action, had seen all that Biggles had seen. In fact, he had seen more, for so far he was unmolested, and flying on a straight course towards the canal, was able to get a clear view of it. From a distance he had seen Biggles's bombs explode, and, shortly afterwards, the destruction of the end shed. He had watched the archie barrage following him, and then return with renewed violence to the area in which Algy in the *Didgeree-Du* was now taking up the fight. He saw, too, the explosion of Algy's bombs, although by this time he himself was preparing for action.

The wisdom of Biggles's plan was now apparent, for not only was he down to a thousand feet, but he had been able to line his machine up with the sheds, which he could see clearly in the lurid glow of the fires, without his presence being suspected.

This satisfactory state of affairs, however, was not to last. Trembling a little with excitement in spite of his efforts to remain calm, he had commenced a shallow dive towards the objective when a searchlight suddenly swung round and flashed on his wings. It overshot him, and before it could turn back he had steepened his dive so that it sought him in vain. Nevertheless, the damage had been done, and in a twinkling the other lights were probing the air around him.

His mouth turned dry as the first archie shells lacerated the air dangerously close to him. He knew they were close because he could hear the muffled explosions above the roar of his engine, and Biggles had told him that archie was only dangerous when close enough to be heard. He had expected the barrage to be bad, but not quite as terrifying as this. Several times he felt splinters strike the *Dingo*, and although he tried hard not to think about it, his imagination refused to be side-tracked so easily. However, he kept his eyes on the sheds, determined to get a direct hit or die in the attempt. To endure all this danger for nothing was not, he thought, to be borne. Once he caught a glimpse in his reflector of the inferno that raged in the sky behind him, and the muscles of his face went stiff. Still, he reasoned, Biggles had gone through it; so had Algy, therefore, so must he.

An unseen missile crashed through the machine just in front of him with terrifying force. Something struck him on the cheek with the bite of a whiplash, and he grunted with pain. Putting his hand to the place, he stared fascinated by the sight of his own blood. Reaction came swift and strong; and, as so often happens, it took the form, not of fear, but of bitter resentment, and he looked for the target with a personal interest. 'I'll show you,' he muttered furiously, and jammed the stick forward in a kind of fierce exultation.

Down – down – down, he roared, careless now of the storm of fire that raged about him. 'I'm going to get those sheds or bust,' he told himself desperately, and it was no idle boast. A glance at the altimeter gave him a shock, for the needle was nearly on zero; he had not realised that he was so low.

In a sort of daze, feeling that the thing was not really happening and that he would presently wake up, he took aim with calculated deliberation. He was still a little short of the target, and the second or two that he had to wait exasperated his patience. He wanted to see the bomb burst and blow everything sky high.

Slowly, as the wing crept up to the first shed, his hand groped for the bomb-toggle. 'Now,' he muttered, suddenly conscious of a sense of power, and pulled the handle back as far as it would go. The *Dingo* bumped as the steel-clad load of high explosive plunged earthward.

Ginger was torn between a desire to wait and watch what happened and an urge to dive clear; fortunately for him his common sense prevailed, or it is unlikely that he would have lived long enough to know how successful he had been. He had zigzagged away as Biggles had told him, and was about to turn to see the result of his effort when the entire world seemed to blow up, lighting earth and sky in one terrific blaze. He felt the heat of it on his face. The *Dingo*, caught in that fearful blast, soared dizzily, throwing him against the safety-belt with a force that made him gasp. Temporarily blinded and half stunned by shock, he skidded crazily round the sky not knowing which way to go. In a subconscious way he noticed that most of the searchlights had gone out; nor was the archie as bad as it had been. The lattice mast of a wireless tower seemed to leap out of the darkness towards him, and he dragged the stick back into his thigh in a panic. He missed the mast by inches, but the shock did something to restore his senses to normal. 'Gosh! I'm nearly on the ground,' he thought frantically, and made haste to correct the error. He saw the canal, and made for it like a pigeon; for a few seconds he followed it; then, happening to glance at his compass, he saw that he was going the wrong way.

Again it was in something like a panic that he whirled the machine round and sped like a bullet towards the open sea. For some minutes the archie followed him, but in some curious way he had ceased to be alarmed by it. He began to laugh, but pulled himself up abruptly. 'That won't do,' he told himself seriously, and remembering the wound in his face, he felt it carefully. It was still bleeding, but, as far as he could make out, not badly. In any case, he was not conscious of any pain, so he thought no more about it. He did not bother to climb for height, but checking his compass, set about getting home by the shortest possible route. He remembered Biggles and Algy, and wondered vaguely how they had fared, but his thoughts were chaotic and he found it difficult to concentrate. 'I suppose I shall get used to this sort of thing,' he mused philosophically.

He could see the black bulk of Bergen Ait some time before he reached it; indeed, he was surprised that he could see it so plainly. He scanned the sea for ships, but there were none in sight, for which he was thankful, for it permitted him to make straight for the cove.

It was clear when he reached it, but as he glided down he could just make out one of the other machines being towed into the cave. Three flashes of a green light gave him the signal to land, and in a minute or two he was on the water, taxiing towards where he knew the entrance of the cave to be. The *Dingo* seemed strangely sluggish, but he thought nothing of it until the motorboat dashed out, with Briny in the bows making frantic signals to him to hasten. Obediently he gave the engine more throttle, and roared into the cave, where the motorboat took the machine in tow and dragged it to the catwalk.

He switched off and pushed up his goggles. 'What's the matter?' he asked weakly.

Biggles answered. 'You were sinking. You must have got a float holed. It's all right now; the Flight-Sergeant will attend to it.'

Ginger sprang up in alarm. 'Great Scott!' he cried. 'I didn't know.'

Biggles helped him ashore. 'Good work, laddie,' he said patting him on the back, 'you got it a beauty.'

'How did you know?' inquired Ginger. 'Did you see it?'

'I certainly did – that is, I saw the blaze on the sky. They saw it from here – and heard it.'

Ginger stared. 'Well, do you know, that's a funny thing,' he said shakily. 'I was right on top of it yet I didn't hear a blessed thing.' He staggered suddenly.

Biggles caught him. 'Bear a hand, Algy,' he said sharply, noting the blood on Ginger's face. 'He's been hit. He needs medical attention.'

Ginger laughed foolishly. 'Don't you believe it,' he protested, 'what I want is my supper.'

CHAPTER V

An Unwelcome Visitor

For three days the Boomerang Squadron had no further instructions from London, for which Biggles was grateful, for the respite gave him time to organise things at the base to his entire satisfaction, and gave Ginger's face a chance to heal. The wound turned out to be a very slight one, no more than a cut from a flying splinter. Even so, in his excited condition it was enough to give him a temperature, and much to his disgust Biggles ordered him to remain in bed for a day. The period of inactivity also gave the Flight-Sergeant an opportunity of repairing the machines, all of which had been more or less damaged by gunfire.

Only one signal was received, and this could not have been more brief. It consisted of a single word, 'Congratulations'.

'I suppose that's from Colonel Raymond,' said Ginger. 'How do you suppose he knows how much damage we did – when we don't really know ourselves?'

Biggles laughed shortly. 'He knows all right, you can bet your boots on that,' he asserted. 'We've got agents on the spot, I'll warrant. Somebody told me that we had an agent at Kiel right through the last war. Anyway, since

33

Headquarters has gone to the trouble of congratulating us, we must have made a nasty mess of the dump.'

One other item of news interested them immensely, and this they received on the ordinary radio, a powerful instrument on which they could get all the world's programmes. They rarely had time to listen to music, but the news broadcasts kept them up to date on the progress of the war. The item that pleased them most was the story of the raid by R.A.F. Squadrons on the German battleships at the entrance to the Kiel Canal. It had occurred on the same day as their own raid, and Biggles realised that the two raids must have been part of the same plan to destroy the enemy's equipment in the canal zone.

It was late in the morning of the third day after the raid that the next signal was received. The three pilots were sitting in the tiny mess, listening to Briny, who was describing with a wealth of graphic detail a raid in which he had once taken part against the warring tribes of the Solomon Islands.

'Ten thousand of 'em there was, a-dancin' and brandishin' their spears; and only me and my old shipmate Charlie to face 'em,' he declared in a hoarse whisper. '"Charlie," I sez, "you attack 'em in the flank. I'll tackle 'em in front. Charge!" I yells, and you wouldn't believe it—'

'You're quite right, Briny, I wouldn't,' put in Biggles sadly. 'Personally I could charge a well-done steak right now, so—'

Roy hurried into the room with the signal. He saluted and handed it to Biggles who, after a glance at the coded message, took it to the records room, the others following. He unlocked the safe, took out the code-book, and the envelope to which the signal referred.

'They seem to have got our jobs all ready for us before we came,' remarked Algy.

'The Colonel as good as told us so,' reminded Biggles. 'It was only to be expected. Our people have got spies on the mainland, and probably knew before the war started the most vital objectives which could be reached by a unit stationed here.' He read the orders in silence, the others watching his face anxiously.

'Well?' exclaimed Algy at last, impatiently.

Biggles glanced up. 'Listen to this,' he said quietly. '"To Officer Commanding 'Z' Squadron, on detached duty. On the first night after receipt of these instructions on which weather conditions are suitable, you will destroy the tunnel on the Berlin-Hamburg railway at Albeck, about sixty miles from the coast, as shown on the enclosed map. Owing to the depth of the tunnel it is not possible to do this by direct bombing. The only way success can definitely be assured is by placing an explosive charge (case W.D. 6. in your stores) in the tunnel. This will involve landing in enemy territory. A suitable field, one and a quarter miles from the tunnel, is marked in red on the map. You are warned that both ends of the tunnel are guarded day and night by double sentries. The guard-houses are situated as follows. At the northern end, a farm building seventy-eight yards north-east. At the southern end, a signal box twenty-five yards south-south-east. Receipt of these instructions will be acknowledged by a double A transmitted on the wave-length allotted to you three times at intervals of three seconds."'

Biggles finished reading, laid the paper on the desk and tapped a cigarette reflectively on the back of his hand.

'Very pretty,' announced Algy cynically. 'Do they think we possess some means of making ourselves invisible?'

'That's all right, old boy, you needn't come,' murmured Biggles casually.

Algy started forward belligerently. 'What do you mean – I needn't come? You can't leave me out of a show like this—'

'I'm sorry,' broke in Biggles blandly, 'but I rather gathered from your remark that you'd prefer to stay at home.'

'Well, think again,' snorted Algy.

'And that's no way to talk to your commanding officer,' returned Biggles. 'All right. We'll tell Roy to send the acknowledgement and then, with the map in front of us, think of ways and means. As a matter of fact, I did a job like this once before,' he added, as they went to the radio room and gave Roy instructions concerning acknowledgement of the orders.

Roy, with earphones clamped on his head, made a note on his pad. 'By the way, sir, I'm picking up a lot of Morse,' he said. 'I think it's being sent out from somewhere not very far away. It's in code, of course.'

'By jingo, if we could read it, it would be useful!' exclaimed Ginger. 'Do you think we could decode it?'

'Not a hope,' answered Biggles promptly. 'What point would there be in using a code that could be deciphered by the enemy? The only way official messages can be deciphered in war-time is with the official key, and that's something we're not likely to get hold of. I imagine the British government would be only too pleased to pay a million pounds for the German secret code at this moment. All the same, Roy, you can keep a record of any Morse you pick up – one never knows. Get that acknowledgement off right away.'

'Very good, sir.'

Biggles led the way back to the office and spread the map on the table. 'All we can do is memorise the spot,' he said, pointing with his forefinger, 'and work out the best way of getting to it. We shan't need three machines; two should be enough, one to do the job and the other to act as a reserve – and possibly a decoy. I'll think about that. If the weather is O.K. we may as well go tonight and get it over. Algy, go and dig out that box marked W.D. 6. I'll go and have a look at the sky. No,' he added as an afterthought, 'there's no need for me to go. You go, Ginger, while I have a look at the map.'

Leaving Biggles pondering over the map, Ginger made his way along the catwalk. He stopped for a few minutes to speak to the Flight-Sergeant, who was still working on the *Dingo*, and then went on towards the mouth of the cave.

Even before he pulled the tarpaulin aside he was aware, from the shrill cries of the gulls, that something unusual was happening outside. Thinking that possibly the cause was a coming change in the weather, for he knew that gulls often get excited at such times, he moved the heavy tarpaulin and looked out. Instinctively his eyes turned upwards to the birds. Normally the majority sat placidly on the ledges on the face of the cliff, but now they all appeared to be on the wing, and he was amazed at the number of them. The air was full of whirling white forms, thousands of them, wheeling and at the same time uttering discordant cries of alarm.

At first Ginger could see nothing on account of the birds, but as he stared he became aware that they seemed to be concentrating at two places, not very far apart. Focusing his eyes on the spot, he caught his breath sharply as he perceived the reason for the uproar. Two men in dark uniforms were creeping along a ledge; in their hands they carried baskets in which they were putting something which they were picking up from the rocks.

It did not take Ginger long to realise that they were collecting the eggs of the gulls, which were protesting at the outrage in the manner already described. For a full minute he stared at the two men as his brain strove to grasp the significance of their presence. Unprepared for anything of the sort, he was for the moment completely taken aback; but as his composure returned he realised that a boat of some sort must have brought them, and he looked along the foot of the cliffs to locate it. It was not hard to find. It was a small collapsible canoe. Sitting beside it, calmly smoking a pipe, was a third man.

Again Ginger's eyes moved, for he knew that such a frail craft could not have made its way to the rock across the open sea, and what he saw turned him stiff with shock. Lying just off the entrance to the cove, not two hundred yards away, was a submarine, its grey conning-tower rising like a monument above the deck. There was no need to question its nationality, for on the side of the tower was painted, in white, the single letter U. Below it was the number 159.

How long the submarine had been there, Ginger, of course, did not know, but it had evidently been there for some time, for several members of the crew were disposed about the deck, sunning themselves in the autumn sunshine, while a line of washing hung between the conning-tower and a circular gun turret.

Ginger was still staring, half stunned by shock, when he heard a noise inside the cave that galvanised him into frantic activity. It was the swish-swish of an engine as its propeller was turned preparatory to starting, and he knew that Smyth was about to test the *Dingo*. Releasing the tarpaulin which he was still holding, he tore back along the catwalk and nearly knocked the Flight-Sergeant into the water with the violence of his approach. He was just in time, for the Flight-Sergeant's hand was already on the starter.

'Stop!' he gasped. 'Don't make a sound.' Leaving the mechanic gazing after him, as if he had lost his reason, he dashed along to the records room, where he found Biggles and Algy still poring over the map.

Their eyes opened wide at the expression on his face. 'What's wrong?' snapped Biggles.

Ginger pointed down the cave. 'There's a U-boat in the cove,' he panted.

There was dead silence for a moment. Then Biggles sprang to his feet. 'The dickens there is,' he said tersely. 'What's it doing?'

Briefly, Ginger described the situation.

'I'd better have a look,' muttered Biggles. 'There seems to be nothing we can do except sit quiet in the hope that it will soon clear off.'

'Suppose these bird-nesters find the cave?' asked Ginger.

'It'll be the last birds'-nesting they do for a long time,' promised Biggles grimly.

'It's the U 159,' Ginger informed him.

Biggles clenched his fists. 'By thunder,' he swore, 'here's a chance. It was the U 159 that sank the liner *Arthurnia* without warning, so it would be just retribution if we handed it a basinful of the same medicine. It must be on its way back to its depot. Come on.'

He dashed off down the catwalk closely followed by the others, but nearing the tarpaulin he slowed down and peered cautiously round the end of it.

The U-boat was still in the same position, but the men who had been ashore, evidently having filled their baskets, were making their way back in the canoe. Reaching the submarine, they climbed leisurely on board.

'They seem to be in no hurry,' observed Biggles anxiously. 'I'm afraid we're going to have them hanging about for some time. Ginger, send the Flight-Sergeant to me.'

Presently the Flight-Sergeant came at the double, and Biggles gave him orders in a low voice. 'Get an armour-piercing bomb on each machine and cast off ready for instant action.' He turned to the others. 'If she finds the cave we shall have to go for her,' he explained. 'There are probably forty or fifty men on board, so if they once got ashore we shouldn't have a chance. They'd radio our position to Germany, anyway, and probably plaster us with that heavy gun on the bows. Our machine-guns wouldn't be much use against that. I'm still hoping they'll go without finding us.'

An hour passed, and still the submarine gave no indication of departure. Another hour went by; the washing was taken in and the deck cleared, but not until mid-afternoon did the sinister craft begin to turn slowly towards the open sea.

Biggles breathed a sigh of relief. 'She's going,' he said. 'That's the best thing that could happen for everybody.'

With her steel deck awash, the submarine ploughed its way slowly towards the south, the airmen watching it with mixed feelings of relief and regret, for such a mark might never again present itself.

Ginger, who had fetched a pair of binoculars, steadied himself against the rock and brought them into focus. 'How far is it away do you think?' he asked Biggles.

'About a couple of miles – why?'

'It's stopped – at least, I think so. Yes, it has,' declared Ginger. 'There seem to be some officers on deck – they're looking at something on the water. By gosh! It's coming back.'

Biggles grabbed the glasses – not that they were really necessary, for what Ginger had said was obviously correct. The submarine had swung round in a wide circle and was returning over its course.

'What's the idea?' asked Algy. 'What could they have seen to bring them back?'

Biggles snapped his fingers. 'I've got it,' he cried. 'Look!' He pointed at an iridescent stain that drifted from the mouth of the cave and spread in a long wavy line towards the southern horizon. 'They've spotted that oil,' he added sharply. 'They're on their way back to see where it's coming from. It'll bring them straight to the cave. Quick! The machines! We've got to get that sub, or it's all up with us. Pull that tarpaulin out of the way, Smyth.'

There was a rush for the machines. Biggles was away first, as he was bound to be, for the *Willie-Willie* was nearest the entrance and blocked the way of the others. The roar of its engine drowned all other sounds. Leaving a wake of churning water behind it, the machine shot through the entrance to the cave and raced on over the cove. It bumped once or twice as it struck the swell of the open sea, and then, after climbing for a moment or two at a steep angle, made straight for the U-boat.

Biggles knew that there was no time for tactics. In the first place the members of the submarine crew must have heard his engine start, and no doubt they could now see him. That was not all. He knew that he had got to send the U-boat to the bottom before a wireless message could be sent to the shore, or a flotilla of destroyers would be round the islet like a pack of wolves round a wounded deer. It was in an attempt to prevent this happening that Biggles roared straight at the submarine.

From a distance of a quarter of a mile he could see the gun-crew feverishly loading their weapon, and more in the hope of delaying them than hitting anybody, he brought his nose in line and fired a series of short bursts from his machine-guns. Whether it was due to this or an order from the commander he did not know, but the men suddenly abandoned their weapon and bundled into the conning-tower. The top closed and the U-boat began to submerge.

But by this time Biggles was over it. His bomb hurtled down. He zoomed away swiftly, banking steeply on the turn so that he could see what happened. What he saw brought a grim smile to his lips. As quick as he had been, the others were not far behind him. The *Didgeree-du* and the *Dingo*, in line, swept over the patch of swirling water. Two great columns of smoke and spray shot upwards. The stern of the U-boat rose high out of the water, the propellers racing; higher and higher it rose until it was almost vertical; then it plunged downwards and disappeared from sight.

For a little while Biggles continued to circle, the other machines following him, in case there should be any survivors; but there were none, and in his heart he was relieved, for they were in no condition to take care of prisoners. A final glance at the wide patch of oil that marked the last resting-place of the U-boat and he turned back towards the islet. Without waiting for the others to land, he raced straight on into the cave, and, jumping out, ran on to the radio room.

'Did that submarine manage to get out a signal?' he asked Roy sharply.

'Yes, sir. It was very short though – not more than three or four words, I should say, although as they were in code I don't know what they mean. I've got a record of the letters though.'

'I see,' said Biggles slowly, and returned to the catwalk where the others were just coming ashore.

'What you might call short and sweet,' remarked Algy.

'Short, but not very sweet,' answered Biggles. 'Ah, well, that's war. If it hadn't been them it would have been us. That's what they've been handing out to unarmed ships so they could hardly complain. The Admiralty will be glad to know that one raider is out of the way. It seems to be a case where we might risk transmitting a signal. But come on, we'd better get ready for this show tonight.'

CHAPTER VI

A Dangerous Mission

The plan for the blowing up of the Albeck tunnel, as
finally decided by Biggles and accepted without demur by
the others, was completed, and as the weather remained
favourable it was agreed to put it into operation that
night. Two machines would go over, the first to be the
Willie-Willie converted into a two-seater, with Biggles and
Ginger in it. This was actually the operative aircraft. It
would carry the explosive charge – a time bomb – with
which they hoped to destroy the tunnel, and fly at its
maximum ceiling, which Biggles thought could not be
less than 25,000 feet. This would, of course, involve the
use of oxygen apparatus, which had not been overlooked
by the Admiralty in fitting out the base. Algy, in the
Didgeree-du, also converted into a two-seater, was to take
off twenty minutes after the others and fly at 10,000 feet
with a dual role to play. Primarily, his purpose was to
act as a decoy to distract attention from the operative
machine by drowning the noise of its engine with its own.
Secondly, it could act as a reserve plane to pick up the
occupants of the first machine if by any chance it should
be damaged in landing. If its services were required Biggles
would signal to it by means of a red light; otherwise, it was
to return home independently.

Biggles saw clearly that the greatest difficulty to be overcome was to reach the landing-field undetected, for it was too far inland to be reached in a glide after the manner adopted in the attack on the ammunition dump. He knew that if once the machine was picked up by the ever-questing searchlights it would not only be futile to land, but suicidal; so, after giving the matter considerable thought, he had decided on the scheme just outlined as the most likely way of escaping observation. Algy was to fly straight towards the landing-field, drawing both the searchlights and the anti-aircraft gunfire. In this way it was hoped that the other machine, flying 15,000 feet above it, would, by cutting its engine some distance away, be able to reach the field more or less silently. Once the *Willie-Willie* was on the ground matters would have to take their course. Biggles would have to open his engine in order to get off again, but this he did not mind, trusting to his ability to get back in the face of anything the enemy might do to prevent it.

To start with, the watches of both machines would be synchronised; both aircraft were to rendezvous over the islet at a prearranged time, at their respective altitudes, and fly on the same compass course at the same speed. This should (as Biggles explained) keep them together, for they would not be able to see each other. He, having to climb to a greater height, would take off first. The scheme was not entirely satisfactory, but he was convinced that it was the best they could do in the circumstances.

'We'll start as soon as it's dark,' he concluded. 'It may take us some time to get into the tunnel, and it wouldn't do to be caught out in daylight.'

Accordingly, the machines were made ready, and at nine p.m. the *Willie-Willie*, with Biggles in the pilot's seat and Ginger crouching over a gun behind him, taxied out to the cove. Another minute and they were in the air, spiralling steadily upwards.

For twenty minutes the steel airscrew of the *Willie-Willie* clawed its way into the starlit heavens, by which time the altimeter needle registered 22,000 feet, and the airmen adjusted their oxygen apparatus; then, still climbing slightly, Biggles struck off to the south-west at a steady speed of 280 miles an hour. Half an hour later the German mainland appeared ahead, black, sinister, as mysterious as another world. A finger of gleaming silver stabbed the darkness, and soon the air was cut into sections by the ever-alert searchlights.

Biggles's voice reached Ginger over the telephone. 'Look down,' he said. 'Poor old Algy seems to be copping it.'

Ginger looked over the side. Far below, so far that they appeared to be on the ground, a hundred flickering points of light danced in the darkness, and he knew it was the archie barrage throwing a curtain of fire round Algy's machine. It was hard to believe that the bursting shells were 10,000 feet above the earth. For a time he watched the barrage moving along below them, and from it was able to judge roughly the position of the *Didgeree-du*. Algy was getting the worst of it now, he reflected, but their turn would come later.

Once a probing beam swept perilously close to the *Willie-Willie*, but Biggles side-slipped away, sacrificing a little height in the slip, but keeping on his course.

The minutes passed; one by one the searchlights went out and the barrage thinned, as the coastal batteries were left behind. Below, the earth was wrapped in profound darkness, but the roads showed dimly, like pale threads snaking across the vast panorama. Woods and forests showed as inky stains on the vague background of the earth. Occasional flashes still followed the course of Algy's machine, and the cunning of Biggles's plan became apparent, for so far not a single shell had come near the *Willie-Willie*, and it seemed fairly certain that its presence had not been suspected by the watchers on the ground. Shortly afterwards the archie trail swung away to the left, and Ginger knew that Algy had begun to circle away in accordance with their plan. That Biggles had noticed it, too, was made apparent when the *Willie-Willie's* engine died, leaving the machine to glide silently along its lonely course.

Standing up to look immediately below them, Ginger saw what he expected to find – the railway; a long straight line that began in the indistinct distance behind them and vanished into the black horizon ahead. He considered it seriously, knowing that Biggles's skill in pilotage would now be severely tested, for to bring a machine down from such a height on a given landing-ground, at night, without touching the throttle, required more skill than the average pilot possessed.

Once a curious, nebulous ball of fire rolled along the line, and he knew that it must be a train; the lights in the carriages were out, but the fireman could not prevent the glow from reflecting on the smoke as he stoked his furnace.

Ginger thought the glide would never end. It seemed interminable, the more so because, owing to their great height, they did not appear to be moving; nor did they seem to get any lower, although he knew that this was not the case, for the altimeter told a true story and the needle was swinging back all the time.

Staring fixedly ahead, he saw the thin line of the railway end abruptly, as if it were cut off short in open country, and he knew they had at last reached the tunnel. A moment later the machine began a wide, flat spiral, and the details on the ground soon showed up more clearly. The moon had risen, and in its cold blue light he could even see the farm-building at the northern end of the tunnel which he knew must be the guard-house.

Quickly now the greys became less dim, and the outlines of woods and hedges stood out more sharply. A wide river, which he knew must be the Elbe, meandered across a deserted landscape to the north-west, for villages were few and far between.

A current of air on his left cheek interrupted his survey as the machine went into a steep side-slip, and he realised that Biggles must have arrived over the objective with plenty of height to spare; he noted it with satisfaction, for had they undershot they could only have reached the landing-ground by opening the engine. Looking ahead he could see it, a large field roughly triangular in shape, with a group of trees at the apex. He glanced at Biggles, and saw that he was leaning forward as he operated the gear that lowered the undercarriage wheels.

The field was under them now. Almost imperceptibly the nose of the machine came up as Biggles flattened out. The tail sank a little, but still the machine glided on towards the trees, its wheels about two feet above the grass.

Ginger held his breath and waited, praying that there were no unseen obstacles, for on the floor of his cockpit rested a small, square wooden case containing enough high explosive to blow the machine to atoms. He breathed again as the wheels touched, bumped gently once or twice, and trundled on towards the trees. He felt the machine strain slightly as the left wheel brake was applied, causing the aircraft to swing slightly so that it finished its run a dozen yards from the trees, facing the open field ready for an instant take-off should danger threaten. Silence fell.

'Well, here we are,' remarked Biggles quietly.

'Nice work, chief,' acknowledged Ginger.

They both got out of the machine, Ginger taking the explosive charge with him, and stood still, listening, peering with straining eyes into the dim moonlight, for there was just sufficient light for it to be deceptive.

'Everything seems to be quiet; I don't think we were spotted,' said Biggles at last. 'Give me a hand.'

Slowly, and not without effort, they dragged the machine back into the dense gloom under the trees, leaving it with its nose still pointing to the open field. There was no movement of air, so the question of the direction of the wind did not arise.

'Good! She'll do nicely there. We'll get along,' muttered Biggles softly, and picking up the time-bomb, set off down a hedge that led in the direction of the tunnel.

They came to a gap, and crawling through it, came out in a lane, which they followed for some distance; then Biggles cut across country, keeping as close as possible to the hedges, until they came to a slight embankment. 'We're about over the tunnel,' whispered Biggles. 'If we turn right here it should bring us to the entrance.'

In a quarter of an hour, now moving slowly and with infinite caution, they came within sight of the railway line. Lying flat, Biggles surveyed the scene. There was no one in sight. The guard-house, a square black barn, stood about a hundred yards away, but of the sentries there was no sign. He crept forward for a short distance and again lay still, straining his eyes to find the men who he knew must be there.

He was still staring into the tricky half-light when the door of the barn was suddenly thrown open; a shaft of yellow light fell athwart the grass, and a peremptory voice, in German, called, 'Keep your eyes open there; there's been an air-raid warning.'

'*Jawohl*,' was grunted in answer, so close to where he lay that Biggles instinctively stiffened.

The door was closed and the light disappeared. Silence returned. But it did not last long. 'Did you hear that, Fritz?' said the voice that had last spoken.

'*Ja*,' came the reply, heavy with boredom, some distance away. 'Anybody would think that the Englanders were coming here. The corporal's nervous. He ought to go into the trenches for a bit; that'd cure him.'

Biggles smiled grimly and felt for Ginger. 'I shall have to knock this fellow on the skull,' he breathed. 'If he makes one sound we're sunk. Keep close to me.' He drew his revolver, and holding it by the barrel, began to creep forward. He had not far to go. A round forage-cap appeared silhouetted against the sky. Beside it, at an angle, was the black outline of a bayonet.

For several minutes Biggles lay still, trying to work out the best way of approach, for there seemed to be a low growth of brambles between him and the sentry, and to cross these without making a sound was manifestly impossible. He was still lying there when, from far away, came the drone of an aero-engine, its steady purr punctuated by the dull *whoof, whoof, whoof,* of archie. He knew that it was Algy, still cruising about watching for a possible signal.

'Hello, Fritz, here comes the Englander,' called the sentry excitedly. 'Come here, you'll see better.'

The last word died on the man's lips, for knowing that if the two sentries came together his task would be infinitely more difficult, Biggles had risked all on a desperate chance. The sound of the man's voice deadened the slight crunch of briars as Biggles crept swiftly across them, added to which the sentry's interest was entirely absorbed by the approaching aircraft. He was staring up into the sky when Biggles rose like a black shadow behind him and brought the butt of his revolver down on his head. The man dropped without a sound.

Tight lipped with anxiety, Biggles whipped off the man's cap and put it on his own head. Snatching up the rifle, with the bayonet fixed, he rose erect just as the second sentry came over the brow of the slope not half a dozen paces away.

'Ah, there you are,' grunted the German as he came on. 'What are you doing?'

Biggles dropped the point of the bayonet until it was a foot from the man's breast. 'One sound and you die,' he said sharply in German, and there was a vibrant quality in his voice that confirmed his dire threat. 'Drop your rifle,' he added.

After his first gasp of astonishment the man made no sound. The rifle fell to the ground with a thud.

'Now lie down on your face and you will not be hurt,' commanded Biggles.

The man obeyed.

'Ginger, pull his greatcoat over his head and tie it round his neck with the belt,' went on Biggles. 'Now tie his wrists behind his back with your handkerchief – pull it tight.' He opened the flap in the butt of the rifle and took out the cord pull-through used for cleaning the barrel of the weapon. Kneeling, he wound it twice round the sentry's ankles and knotted it.

Now these operations had taken perhaps two minutes, and all the time the aeroplane had been drawing nearer. And that was not all. The door of the barn had been thrown open, and half a dozen men poured out, talking excitedly, staring up at the sky. A telephone bell jangled. As if this were not enough, the rumble of a train could be heard approaching the southern end of the tunnel.

Biggles snatched up the time-bomb. 'If either of these fellows moves hit him on the head,' he said grimly. 'If those guards come this way, leave me; make for the machine and save yourself.' Before Ginger could answer he had scrambled down the slope and disappeared into the tunnel.

With his heart beating painfully from suppressed excitement, Ginger squatted beside the sentries, watching the men outside the barn, for in them lay the greatest danger. Once one of them shouted something, presumably to the sentries, but as Ginger could not speak German he did not know what was said, and could only remain silent. Overhead, the aircraft was now turning for home.

Ginger waited. A minute passed; it seemed an eternity of time. Another minute went by. What on earth was Biggles doing, he wondered feverishly? If he wasn't quick he would be knocked down by the train. Then, to add to his panic, one of the men outside the barn detached himself from the group and hurried down the line towards him.

Ginger drew his revolver and curled his finger round the trigger. Why didn't Biggles come?

The man gave a shout and broke into a sprint, and the next instant the reason revealed itself. Biggles came panting up the embankment. 'Run for it,' he gasped.

The man on the line shouted again. It was answered by others. A shot rang out.

'Keep going,' panted Biggles, as they tore through the brambles and made for the hedge that led in the direction of the landing-ground.

Ginger, snatching a glance over his shoulder, saw a line of figures on the top of the embankment, but the next second he was flung flat on his face as the ground rocked to the roar of an explosion that nearly burst his eardrums. Dazed, he staggered to his feet. Biggles caught him by the arm. 'Keep going,' he said again.

If there was a pursuit Ginger saw no more signs of it. His knees were weak under him by the time they reached the field in which the plane had been left. Gasping for breath, for they had crossed a ploughed field and their boots were caked with mud, he staggered on. Biggles, too, was puffed, and had to slow down. The group of trees that concealed the machine was still some distance away, but they plodded on, keeping close to the hedge. Once an aeroplane, its navigation lights ablaze, roared over them.

'They've got fighters up, looking for Algy I suppose,' panted Biggles. 'They'll be after us, too, presently,' he added, as they reached the machine, still standing as they had left it.

'Have *we* got navigation lights on?' asked Ginger suddenly. 'I forgot to look.'

'Yes – why?'

'Then why not switch 'em on and fly low?'

Biggles stared. 'Have you gone crazy?'

'I shouldn't be surprised, but I was thinking that they would take us for one of themselves and leave us alone.'

Biggles laughed aloud as he scrambled into his seat. 'Brilliant idea,' he declared. 'We can always switch the lights off if the dodge doesn't work. Come on – let's go.'

Ginger climbed into his seat; the machine raced across the dew-soaked turf and in a few moments was in the air, heading northward.

As soon as they were at a thousand feet Biggles switched on the navigation lights, clearly revealing their position to anyone on the ground. He was only just in time, for a searchlight beam was already feeling its way towards them; but as the lights came on it swung away so as not to dazzle (as the operator evidently thought) the pilot of one of his own machines.

Ginger chuckled. The scheme was working. Indeed, it worked far better than they could have hoped, for not once were they challenged either by searchlights or anti-aircraft guns. They had one shock, and that was when an enemy machine, also carrying lights, came close to them, and actually flew for a short distance beside them. But apparently the deception was not suspected by the pilot of the German plane, for presently it turned away and disappeared into the night.

As they crossed the coastline Ginger let out a yell of triumph. Biggles did not answer, and leaning forward to see why, Ginger saw him staring ahead with a tense expression on his face, revealed in the luminous glow of the instruments. 'What's wrong?' he cried.

Biggles's answer was terse. 'I may be wrong, but that looks like fog ahead.'

Hardly had the words left his lips when a wisp of clammy moisture clutched at the machine, and the next instant everything was blotted out.

With his eyes on his instruments, Biggles switched off the navigation lights, which could no longer serve them, and easing the stick back, started to climb. He knew that it was no use trying to get under the fog, for he was already flying so low that to fly lower would be dangerous. There was just a chance, however, that if the fog proved to be no more than ground mist he might be able to get above it and see through it; for it is a curious fact that what at a low altitude may be an opaque blanket, can become transparent from a great height. But when the *Willie-Willie* had climbed to 5,000 feet, and was still fogbound, he knew that height would not help them; still he went on climbing, and shortly afterwards emerged into a cold, tranquil world of utter loneliness, beautiful in a way, but almost terrifying in its desolation. Overhead, the moon and stars gleamed in the dark blue vault of heaven, throwing a silvery sheen on the ocean of cloud that lay below, an expanse as flat as an Arctic snowfield, stretching as far as the eye could see. Just above it roared the *Willie-Willie*, with its shadow, surrounded by a misty halo, keeping it company.

With his eyes on the compass Biggles flew on. Half an hour passed and he knew that they must be somewhere near their base, but no break appeared in the all-concealing blanket that lay below. He dare not go down now for fear of colliding with the rock, so he started to circle, hoping to find a break in the fogbank; but it was in vain.

Two courses now lay open to him. Either he could turn away from the base, and, flying by instruments, endeavour to put the *Willie-Willie* down on the open sea, or he could continue circling in the hope that the fog would disperse before his petrol ran out. This, however, was unlikely, for he had only an hour's petrol left, and he knew from experience that the fog would probably persist until it was banished by the rising sun. If the fog did not disperse, then in an hour he would have to go down anyway, so he decided to go down while there was still petrol in his tanks; otherwise, even if he did get down safely, he would find himself adrift on hostile waters.

The steady roar of the engine died away as he cut the throttle and raised the landing wheels that would not again be needed; at the same time he pushed the joystick forward. With the air humming a mournful dirge through the slowly rotating propeller, the machine glided down to the silvery plain that seemed to stretch to eternity, as smooth and level as a frozen sea. For a few seconds the floats ploughed into it, tearing it up like cotton wool; then the fog took the machine into its clammy grip.

Biggles sat quite still, his eyes on the altimeter needle. Minutes passed, minutes as long as hours, while the needle crept back round the dial – 4,000... 3,000... 2,000... 1,000. Still the gloom persisted. The acid test was now to begin. The needle continued its backward revolution, quivering slightly, over the hundred-feet mark.

Biggles had this advantage. He was not landing on unknown country where there was a risk of colliding with a hill, a high building, or trees. He had set the altimeter at sea-level, and to sea-level they were returning. He could, therefore, fly to fine limits.

Inexorably the needle sank, ticking off the hundred marks on the dial. Biggles had pushed up his goggles and was leaning over the side of the cockpit, blinking the moisture off his eyelashes as he stared down into the void. Two hundred feet, and there was still no sign of the black water which he knew was there; a hundred...

Ginger held his breath and braced himself for the shock which he felt was inevitable. The altimeter needle came to rest on the pin. Zero! Simultaneously a dark indistinct mass loomed up below.

The machine flattened out as Biggles snatched the stick back and held it level. The dark mass disappeared, returned, and then showed as black as ink. Biggles pulled the stick right back into his stomach. The *Willie-Willie* lurched sickeningly, and then sank bodily. Splash! A cloud of spray rose into the air. For half a minute the machine forged on, drenching itself with water. Then it came to rest. Biggles flicked off the ignition switch; the propeller stopped its rhythmic ticking. Silence fell. Silence utter and complete.

He unfastened his safety belt. 'Well, we are at least on the floor,' he said philosophically.

'So what?' asked Ginger.

'We sit here until the fog lifts,' returned Biggles. 'We can't do anything else. I only hope Algy got home before all this muck came down.'

CHAPTER VII

Combat!

For some time Biggles sat on the back of his cockpit, deep in thought. Actually, he was doing mental arithmetic, going over in his mind the course he had flown, trying to work out roughly how near – or how far – they were from the base. After a while he gave it up, realising that even if they knew the direction of the islet it would be a most hazardous business trying to get into the cove. The chances were that they would run on the rocks at the foot of the cliff – or be carried on to them by the swell; and even if they managed to secure a handhold, the idea of trying to climb the cliff was not to be considered. It looked impossible in daylight, let alone on a foggy night. The thing that worried him most was that he did not know how fast or in what direction they were drifting. That they were drifting he had no doubt whatever, for there are few places on any ocean entirely free from currents. A four-knot current to the south might, when the fog lifted, leave them in full view of enemy coastguards, with consequences that could hardly fail to be tragic.

His reverie was interrupted by Ginger, who had climbed out and was standing on one of the floats. 'What the dickens is this thing in the water?' he said.

Biggles had been vaguely aware that the machine had jarred slightly against some floating object, but thinking that it was only a piece of driftwood he had paid no attention to it. He joined Ginger on the float, and, without speaking, stood staring at a round object that was just awash.

'That's the third one of those things we've passed,' said Ginger in a puzzled voice.

'What do you mean – we've passed?' asked Biggles sharply.

'What I say.'

'But the thing, whatever it is, must drift at the same rate as ourselves, so how could we pass it? It must be the same one—'

He broke off, and groping under his leather flying coat, took a box of matches from his jacket pocket. A match flared up, casting a small circle of yellow, misty light. 'Good heavens!' he cried aghast as he peered forward at the object. 'It's a mine. We've either come down in a minefield or we've drifted into one.'

The mystery was now explained. They were drifting, but the mines were stationary because they were anchored.

Ginger dropped on his knees and fended the mine away from the float, actually holding it by one of the horns, contact with which might have caused it to explode. 'For the love of Mike let's get clear of the infernal thing,' he muttered desperately.

Biggles said nothing, but he knelt beside Ginger on the float and helped him to push the machine clear.

'What can we do about it?' questioned Ginger.

'Nothing. This knocks any idea of taxiing on the head. We've only got to bump into one of these things – once.

We can't move till daylight, that's certain.' Biggles lit a cigarette and smoked it reflectively.

The night wore on. Several times they saw mines and frequently had to fend the machine clear; but at last came a long interval when they saw none, and Biggles expressed a hope that they were clear of the minefield.

'What's the time?' asked Ginger.

Biggles climbed to the cockpit and looked at the watch on the instrument board. 'Three o'clock.'

'And it won't start to get light until half-past six.'

'About that,' agreed Biggles.

'How far do you reckon we're away from the base?' was Ginger's next question.

'I've no idea,' admitted Biggles. 'We've no indication of how fast we're drifting. I think we must be some way away from the island though, because of these mines. I can't think of any reason why there should be a minefield near the islet. That doesn't mean that the Boche hasn't got a reason, though.'

After that they fell silent again. What seemed to be an eternity of time passed; they could do nothing but sit still and watch for mines, although as a considerable period had passed since they had seen one, it looked as if Biggles's surmise that they were clear was correct.

It was, Ginger judged, about six o'clock when he heard a faint sound in the distance. He noticed that Biggles had evidently heard it too, for he stood up, listening, staring in the direction from which it had come. 'What did that sound like to you?' he asked.

'It sounded like a whistle,' answered Ginger. 'I suppose it isn't possible that we've drifted near the island, and that's—'

'No. Smyth wouldn't whistle if he was looking for us. He'd hail. Hark!'

'I can hear an engine,' asserted Ginger.

'So can I. It's coming towards us, too.'

'Is it the motorboat?'

'No – the beat is too heavy. Great heavens! Look out, it's nearly on us.'

It seemed as if at that moment the fog lifted slightly, for suddenly the muffled beat of powerful engines became clear and strong. Biggles flung himself into the cockpit, and then hesitated. He knew that if they remained where they were they were likely to be run down; on the other hand, if he started the engine the noise would drown all other sounds, and they were likely to collide with the very thing they sought to avoid. A swift glance over his shoulder showed him that Ginger was in his seat. Simultaneously the deep-throated boom of a ship's siren shattered the silence.

Biggles waited for no more. He started the engine, and began taxiing away from the point from which the sound had seemed to come. Hardly had the aircraft got under way when a towering black shape loomed over it. Biggles jerked the throttle wide open and the machine plunged forward. Even so, he thought it was too late, for they were right under the bows of the vessel. He flinched as it bore down on them, and the next instant what appeared to be a monster as large as a cathedral was gliding past them, leaving the plane careering wildly on the displaced water. Above the noise of his engine Biggles heard a bell clanging, and a hail, but he did not stop, for he knew that any ship in those waters was almost certain to be an enemy. A searchlight blazed suddenly, a spectral beam through which the fog swirled like smoke.

By this time the *Willie-Willie* was tearing over the water as fast as Biggles dare take it, for the wake of the huge vessel, which he realised from the searchlight must be a warship, was catching them broadside on, threatening to capsize the comparatively frail aircraft. He could see nothing; even the ship had once more been swallowed up by the fog, and the searchlight with it. For perhaps five minutes he went on; then, satisfied that they were clear, he throttled back, leaving the propeller ticking over. Slowly the machine came to rest and he stood up in his seat. 'Jumping halibut,' he muttered irritably, 'this is getting a bit too much of a good thing.'

'What was it, anyway?' asked Ginger in a strained voice.

'A Boche cruiser I think,' replied Biggles. 'It was going dead slow on account of the fog, or it would have cut us in halves. The lookout saw us, too, but I doubt if they could make out our identification marks, so they would naturally assume that we were one of their own machines, forced down by the fog.'

'In that case they'll probably stop and look for us.'

'They may stop, but I don't think they'll do much looking in this murk. They're more likely to try to give us their position, supposing that we are only too anxious to be picked up. There they go,' he added, as the bellow of a siren boomed across the water.

For half an hour the cruiser remained in the vicinity, sending out frequent blasts; but at the end of that time the eerie sound grew fainter and fainter, and finally ceased altogether – much to Biggles's relief, for the fog was beginning to turn grey with the coming of daylight.

Nevertheless, some time was yet to pass before visibility began to improve. Not for nearly an hour did the luminous white disk of the sun appear, low down on the eastern horizon, to prove that the fog was lifting. Slowly the area of dark-green water round the *Willie-Willie* widened, until it was possible to see a mile in every direction. Knowing that it was now only a matter of minutes before the mist would disperse altogether, Biggles took off and began climbing for height. As he expected, it was possible to see through the fast-thinning vapour, and presently he made out the black mass of Bergen Ait, far to the north-west. He headed towards it and glided down in the cove just as Algy was preparing to take off in search of them.

'I thought you were goners,' he said.

'You'd have thought so if you'd been with us, and that's a fact,' returned Biggles, who was staring at the water in the cove, where a number of seabirds were flapping, as if they found it difficult to get off. Streaks of bright colour showed everywhere. 'Where did all this oil come from?' he asked.

'From the submarine, I imagine,' answered Algy. 'There's oil all over the place.'

'Ah – of course; I forgot.'

'It wasn't only oil that drifted here from the submarine,' went on Algy. 'One of our bombs must have fairly split it in halves, and I fancy the skipper must have been in the act of sending a signal – at least, a whole lot of papers have drifted here. Take a look at this.' He pointed to a book bound in blue oilskin that lay on a rock, with stones between the pages so that the air could dry them.

Biggles took one look at it. 'Sweet spirit of Icarus!' he gasped, slowly turning the pages. 'It's the German secret code. We shall have to let the Admiralty know about this. What a stroke of luck. Hark!'

For a few seconds they all stood motionless in a listening attitude. Then Biggles took a pace forward, staring up at the sky, now a pale eggshell blue. One tiny black speck broke its pristine surface, a speck that grew rapidly in size. Nobody spoke, for they all recognised it. It was a German Dornier flying-boat.

'Get under cover everybody,' ordered Biggles.

He turned and darted along the catwalk towards the signals room, but in a few minutes he was back at the mouth of the cave where the others were still watching the movements of the enemy aircraft through a hole in the tarpaulin. 'It's looking for the submarine we sank yesterday morning,' he said. 'It has sent out several signals; Roy picked them up and I've just decoded them. Incidentally, you were right about the sub; it was signalling when our bombs hit it.'

'The Dornier's coming this way,' observed Algy from the tarpaulin.

Biggles joined him. 'You're right,' he said.

'He's coming lower, too. I'm afraid he's spotted the oil – yes, by gosh, he has. He's coming right down to have a closer look at it. If he follows it to this rock we're sunk.' He stepped back as the Dornier suddenly dived towards the cove. The roar of its engines vibrated through the cave.

'He's going to circle the island,' declared Ginger, with alarm in his voice.

'If the wireless operator starts tapping out a message about the oil there'll be a destroyer here in a brace of shakes,' muttered Biggles. 'Even if he doesn't signal he's bound to report it when he gets back, which will mean the same thing. They are bound to send some sort of boat out to see where the oil is coming from. I'm afraid we've got to stop this chap getting back.' He turned and ran along the catwalk to where the *Willie-Willie* was moored. 'Briny, get that tarpaulin down!' he yelled as he cast off.

The others had followed him along the catwalk. 'I'm coming!' shouted Algy, jumping into his machine.

'Please yourself; the more there are of us the better chance we shall have of getting him. Once we show ourselves we've *got* to get him.'

Biggles's final words were drowned in the roar of his engine, and the *Willie-Willie* surged towards the entrance. To Briny, who was dragging back the tarpaulin, he shouted, 'Where is he?'

'Round the other side of the rock, sir,' bawled Briny.

'Which way did he go?'

'Round to the left.'

Biggles waited for no more; he shoved the throttle open and the *Willie-Willie* tore across the cove in a cloud of spray. Another moment and it was off the water, banking steeply to the left.

Biggles's object was, of course, to come up behind the German plane, which he assumed – from the information Briny had given him – was still circling the island in a left-hand direction. He was, therefore, unprepared for what happened next. Actually, Briny's information had been correct, but what he could not be expected to know was that the Dornier had turned about on the far side of the island and was now coming back towards him. The result was that Biggles, rounding the towering black shoulder of the central mass, nearly collided with him. Both pilots saw each other at the same moment; both banked vertically, and in a split second had raced past each other in opposite directions, before there was even time to think of shooting.

With a grunt of annoyance Biggles dragged the *Willie-Willie* round in its own length, and tore along after the Dornier, just in time to see Algy's machine whirl into sight, and nearly meet the Dornier head on, as he had done.

The enemy pilot – wisely, perhaps, seeing that he was outnumbered – put his nose down for speed and streaked away to the south with the two British machines in hot pursuit.

As he roared low over the cove Biggles glanced down, and seeing no sign of Ginger's machine, wondered where it was. An instant later he knew, for it suddenly flashed into sight across the Dornier's bows. There was a streak of tracer bullets, and then the Dornier went on, apparently unaffected.

What had happened was this. In his desperate haste to get off Ginger had not thought of asking Briny which way the Boche had gone, so instead of turning to the left like the others, he had turned to the right, and in so doing had actually done what the others had intended doing. He had found himself behind the Dornier – in fact, behind all three machines; but as they had dived he found himself above them, and was thus able to use his superior height to gain speed and intercept the machine with the black crosses on its wings. He had managed to get in a short burst of fire at it, but his shooting had been hurried, and it was with chagrin that he saw the Dornier proceed on its way, apparently untouched by his bullets. All he could do was join in the pursuit with the others.

Biggles had no doubts about overhauling the Dornier, for their machines were built for speed whereas the flying-boat was designed primarily for coastal reconnaissance. And since it was soon apparent that they were, in fact, catching it, he had little doubt as to the ultimate result. What upset him was the thought that at that very moment the German wireless operator might be tapping out, as fast as he could, the circumstances of the combat – with, of course, the position of the secret base.

The German pilot did all that he could do against three opponents, as did his gunner, who, facing the pursuers, made things very uncomfortable for them. But he could not shoot in three directions at once, for Biggles and Algy were old hands at the game. At a signal from Biggles they separated to press their attack from different directions. Algy, coming within range, opened fire, drawing the gunner's fire upon himself and so giving Biggles a clear field.

The end came suddenly. Biggles swooped like a hawk and poured in a long decisive burst. He held his fire until collision seemed inevitable and then zoomed high, turning on the top of the zoom to see the result of his attack. Not that he had much doubt as to what it would be. With eight guns pouring out bullets at a rate of a thousand rounds a minute, the Boche must have been riddled.

His supposition was correct. The Dornier was roaring straight up like a rocketing pheasant; for perhaps two seconds it hung on the top of its stall, its airscrews whirling; then its nose whipped down in a spin from which it never recovered. Biggles watched it dispassionately, for he had seen the end of too many combats to be disturbed in his mind; and he was too wise to take his eyes off his victim in case the spin was a ruse to deceive him. That the Dornier was not shamming, however, was confirmed when, with its engine still racing, it plunged nose first into the sea. It disappeared from sight instantly and did not reappear; only an ever widening circle of oil marked the spot where it had ended its fatal dive.

Cutting his engine, Biggles glided down, and circled for some minutes in case there should be a survivor, but it was soon clear that the crew had perished in the machine, so he turned towards the island, anxious to find out from Roy if the radio operator in the Dornier had succeeded in getting out a message.

A glance over his shoulder revealed the others taking up formation behind him, so he went on towards the base, now about six miles distant.

Before he was halfway there Algy had rushed up beside him, beckoning furiously and jabbing downwards with his gloved hand.

Looking down, Biggles saw the reason. Ginger was no longer in the formation; he was gliding down towards the sea, which could only mean one thing – that he was having trouble with his engine. They could not leave him, so Biggles throttled back and began circling down, at the same time throwing a worried glance at the sky, the colour of which promised a change in the weather. He watched Ginger put his machine down on the water, and from its jerky movements saw what he already suspected – that the sea was getting rough. However, he landed within hail of the *Dingo*. 'What's wrong?' he called.

Ginger stood up in his cockpit, holding the edge to steady himself, for the machine was rocking dangerously. 'My engine has cut out,' he shouted. 'It began to splutter after they shot at me.'

Biggles taxied closer, while Algy continued to circle low overhead.

'What shall I do?' asked Ginger.

Biggles thought swiftly. To make repairs on the water was obviously out of the question. Had the sea been calm he would have dashed back to the base and sent the motorboat out to tow the *Dingo* in, but low, ominous clouds were scudding across the sky and the sea was rising quickly. In the circumstances he decided to attempt to tow the *Dingo* in himself. 'Catch this line and make it fast!' he yelled, and swung his mooring-rope across the nose of the *Dingo*.

Ginger caught the line and made it fast to his axle strut, and scrambled back into his seat as Biggles started taxiing towards the base.

Before they had gone a quarter of a mile, however, Biggles knew that they would never reach it, for the sea, now capped with vicious-looking white crests, was throwing both machines about in a manner that was definitely dangerous. A nasty cross-wind was dragging at the *Dingo*, and more than once brought it up short with a jerk on the tow-line that threatened to tear both machines to pieces.

He eased the throttle back, for the question of saving the *Dingo* had become of secondary importance; it was now a matter of saving their lives, for he was by no means sure that he would be able to get the *Willie-Willie* off the water. 'Cut the tow-line!' he yelled. 'Get ready to jump. I'm coming round to pick you up.'

Ginger obeyed the orders unquestioningly, although he realised that they implied the loss of his machine. Climbing out of his seat, he clung to a float, waiting for Biggles to bring the *Willie-Willie* alongside.

It was no easy matter, for both machines were now tossing wildly, and should they be thrown together it would mean the end of them. Blipping his engine, Biggles brought the *Willie-Willie* nearer.

'Jump for it as I go past,' he shouted.

Ginger, balanced on the float, jumped for his life. But his weight, as he jumped, was sufficient to cause the *Dingo* to yaw violently, and instead of landing on Biggles's float, as he hoped, he landed short and disappeared under the water. His head broke the surface almost at once, and he clutched at the float. He managed to grasp it, and endeavoured to drag himself on it, but the weight of his thick, water-soaked clothing held him back.

Seeing his plight, Biggles climbed out, and seizing him by the collar, gave him the assistance he needed. He then helped him into the rear seat.

There was still one more thing to be done. He dared not leave the *Dingo* floating derelict on the water, for not only would it certainly lead to inquiries, but it embodied features which German designers would no doubt be pleased to possess. So as soon as he was back in his cockpit he reached for his signalling pistol, and was taking aim at the *Dingo*'s petrol tank when Algy roared low overhead – so low that it was obvious he was trying to attract attention.

Biggles looked up, and saw Algy's gloved hand jabbing frantically towards the south-east. So occupied had he been with his task that he had paid no attention to the horizon; now, looking in the direction indicated, he saw a sight that brought a scowl to his face. Racing towards them through rain that was beginning to fall was a German destroyer.

CHAPTER VIII

Discoveries

It was typical of him that he finished what he had begun. He took quick aim and sent a flare into the *Dingo's* petrol tank. A tongue of flame spurted out. Satisfied that the destruction of the machine was assured, he pushed his throttle open. Simultaneously a spout of water leapt into the air about fifty yards in front. He had heard the scream of a shell, so he was in no doubt as to what it was. The destroyer, seeing that they were about to escape, had opened fire.

Straight along a trough in the sea roared the *Willie-Willie*, flinging spray high into the air, with spouts of water rising behind it as the German gunners tried in vain to hit the small, fast-moving target. A giant wave loomed up in front, its crest curling ominously, and it was in sheer desperation that Biggles dragged the joystick back, for he knew that the *Willie-Willie* could not meet such a sea head-on and survive. Its floats left the water, and then sank down again as if loath to leave it. They cut through the foaming wave-crest – the machine shuddered and Biggles thought the end had come. An inch lower, and the *Willie-Willie* must have been dragged down, but as it was the crest thrust the machine upward. For a few seconds it hung perilously near a stall; then the racing propeller lifted the nose and it staggered into the air.

Gasping his relief, Biggles looked for Algy, and saw him about a thousand feet above, firing long-range shots at the destroyer – not, of course, with any hope of causing damage, but to irritate the gunners and perhaps spoil their aim. Seeing that Biggles was safely off the water, he desisted, and roared down alongside the *Willie-Willie*.

Biggles, after a last regretful glance at the destroyer – regretful because he had neither bomb nor torpedo with which to attack it – beckoned to Algy and turned his nose to the west with the idea of leading the captain of the enemy ship to think that they were on their way to England. For one thing was certain: under the eyes that he knew would be watching them he dare not return to the base. In any case, with the sea that was by this time running, he doubted if a landing in the cove was possible. So through a mist of driving rain the two machines roared on into the western sky.

Not until he was satisfied that they were out of earshot of the destroyer did Biggles begin turning in a wide curve, for it was not his intention to get a great distance away from the base; indeed, as he had only about an hour's petrol left in his tanks he dare not go far. He was, in fact, in a quandary, and his problem was this: if the rough sea persisted and they returned to the base, it was likely that the machines would be wrecked trying to effect a landing in the cove. By holding on their present course there was just a chance that they might reach a neutral country, in which case, even if they got down safely, they would spend the rest of the war in an internment camp. But they would at least save their lives.

Biggles did not hesitate for long. He decided to return to the island – if he could find it. He was by no means sure that he could, for the weather was fast getting worse. And it continued to get worse, great masses of cloud rolling across the sky and filling the air with a drenching mizzle that blotted everything underneath. Another thing that worried Biggles was the fact that Ginger was already soaked to the skin, and might well collapse from exposure if he remained much longer in the air. How much petrol Algy still had left in his tanks he did not know, but he assumed that it was no more than he himself had. With one thing and another it was in a very anxious state of mind that he began a wide turn which he hoped would bring them within view of the base.

Twenty minutes passed. The wind was now blowing half a gale, bringing with it occasional sleet, and he had to admit to himself that he had no idea of his position. Only one thing was clear, and that was that their condition was little short of desperate; consequently, when a few minutes later he saw land through a hole in the clouds, he lost no time in diving towards it. He knew that it was not Bergen Ait, for it seemed to consist chiefly of a long sandy beach, with flat, marshy ground beyond it; however, since their lives were now at stake, he glided towards it, thankful for the opportunity of getting down anywhere.

As he drew nearer he was able to make out that the beach fringed a large bay, protected on the windward side by rolling sand-dunes, so that the surface of the water, while not by any means calm, was far less rough than the open sea and offered a fair chance of a landing. Had he been sure that the surface of the marsh was firm he would have risked a landing on it, but he had no means of knowing whether it was hard or soft and he dare not take the chance. The only satisfactory thing about the landscape was that it seemed to be entirely deserted, for he could not see a building of any sort.

After a glance over his shoulder to make sure that Algy was following, he glided down to a rather rocky landing, and at once taxied to the shelter of the lee shore, where, after a searching survey of the landscape, he turned to see how Ginger was faring, and to wait for Algy.

Ginger was standing up. His teeth were chattering. 'Crikey!' he muttered, 'isn't it perishing cold! Where are we?'

Biggles shrugged his shoulders. 'Don't ask me. All I know is that we're in a lovely mess – or we shall be if this muck doesn't clear off. Here comes Algy; let's hear what he has to say about it.'

Algy landed and taxied up to them. He pointed to the sandy beach. 'What country's that?' he demanded.

'Search me,' returned Biggles bitterly. 'As far as I'm concerned it could be pretty well anything except Australia or Canada. We've been going round in circles for the last half hour.'

'You're telling me,' snorted Algy. 'You nearly got me dizzy. What made you land here, anyway? Are you thinking of doing a bit of paddling on the beach, or something?'

'If this sea doesn't go down pretty soon you're likely to have all the paddling you want – and bathing too,' retorted Biggles. 'I don't know about you, but my main tank is pretty well dry. We can't do anything about it until the clouds lift – not that I think they will, until this evening. The dickens of it is, Ginger's wet through.'

'Then why not run up on the sand? There ought to be some driftwood about; if there is we could light a fire and warm ourselves.'

Biggles rubbed his chin thoughtfully, a harassed frown lining his forehead. 'If it happens to be a neutral country there'll be a fine old stink if anybody sees us.'

'From what I can see of it there's going to be a stink anyway. I'm all for going ashore.'

'All right,' agreed Biggles. 'If the sand is firm we could take off from the beach.'

No more was said. They taxied the two machines to the edge of the surf, where, lowering their wheels, they ran up on the sand. By the time they had looked about them the rain had stopped, although billowing clouds sweeping low over the sea restricted visibility to about a mile.

'If this stuff will lift a little higher we ought to be able to find our way back to the island,' declared Biggles cheerfully, glancing upward before turning to scrutinise the landscape; but all that could be seen was a long strip of drab yellow sand, unbroken by a footmark and backed by bleak dunes that ended in a fringe of coarse grass. A more desolate spot it would be hard to imagine, for there was not a building of any description in sight, or any other mark of human occupation. Which, of course, suited them very well. There was plenty of driftwood along the high-water mark, so in a short time a brisk fire was burning, with the stranded airmen huddled around it. And there they remained all day, going farther and farther to collect fuel as their stock ran low, noting with satisfaction that between occasional storms the weather slowly improved, with a corresponding extension of visibility.

On one such wood-collecting excursion Ginger found himself near the sand-dunes, so more from a spirit of idle curiosity than definite reconnaissance he climbed to the top of the highest and surveyed the view inland. He discovered that, as not infrequently happens, he could see farther across the landscape than he could over the sea, and thus it was that an unsuspected feature was revealed, a feature that at once explained the desolation. It seemed that they were not on the mainland at all, but on a sand-bank about half a mile wide, and of such length that it could almost claim the description of an island. Beyond it lay a narrow strait, with what he took to be the mainland in the background – a foreshore as low and desolate as the sandbank on which he stood. And he saw something else, something that aroused his curiosity more than a little, although the object was commonplace enough. It was merely a notice-board on the edge of the sandbank; but it seemed to be in a well-kept condition, and he wondered, naturally enough, for what purpose a board should be erected in such a place, since it was hard to imagine that anyone would come there unless compelled to do so – as they had been – by bad weather.

The notice-board stood some distance away, facing the strait, and his curiosity was such that he felt compelled to examine it more closely; at any rate, the language used would tell him what country they had invaded, he reflected; it might even give them the name of the locality, which would be a valuable guide to help them to find the base. So, keeping a careful lookout, he set off across the soaking grass.

The board proved to be at a greater distance than he had judged; however, he encountered no obstacles, and the end of ten minutes' sharp walking saw him standing in front of it.

One glance was sufficient to tell him on whose territory they had landed, for apart from the unmistakable German letters, the order concluded with the two familiar words, 'Heil Hitler'. For the rest, unable as he was to read German, he could only recognise the word *verboten*, which he knew meant forbidden.

He made a note of the text for Biggles's benefit, and was about to start on the return journey when, like a colossal apparition, out of the mist at the northern end of the strait came the last type of vessel he expected to see in such a place. It was a liner, and a huge one at that. He wasted no more time, but bending low, raced back towards the camp as fast as his legs would carry him.

As he topped the last rise he saw Biggles coming to meet him, and Algy's attentive position near the machines suggested that they had become alarmed by his absence.

'What is it?' asked Biggles crisply, knowing from Ginger's attitude that something was amiss.

'We're on an island,' puffed Ginger. 'There's a channel on the other side. There's a whacking great liner going through it.'

Biggles's face expressed amazement, but he dashed up the slope, and throwing himself down, peered through the long grass. 'Well, upon my life, if it isn't the *Leipzig*!' he gasped. 'She's the swell German luxury liner. You remember she disappeared after leaving South America about three weeks ago. The Navy's been scouring the seas for her. So she's got away, after all. I should say she's going to Danzig, now the Germans have captured the city. They'll probably use her as a troopship. What a tragedy we haven't a torpedo with us. What a target she makes! But what's the use of talking. Even if we took off now, and found the base right away, it would be dark before we could get back.'

For some minutes they lay still, watching the great ship creeping majestically down the channel.

'Why were you away so long?' asked Biggles presently.

'I went to have a look at that notice-board over there.'

'Notice-board? Where?'

Ginger pointed. 'There it is. I went to see what was written on it. It's in German, so we're evidently in Germany. The only word I knew was *verboten*, but I made a note of the rest.' He recited the words.

'That simply means "landing forbidden – anyone trespassing will get it in the neck" – or words to that effect.'

'Why should people be forbidden to land on a place like this? Who would want to land, anyway?'

'It's no use asking me,' returned Biggles briefly. 'Wait a minute though,' he added. 'There must be something here people are not allowed to see, and if that is so we ought to find out what it is – although goodness knows what it can be.'

They watched the liner disappear into the mist and then returned to the machines.

Algy greeted them impatiently. 'I reckon we could get off now,' he said, jerking his thumb in the direction of the sky. 'It has started to get dark, so if we hang about much longer we shall have to stay all night.'

'Yes, we'll go,' agreed Biggles. 'All the same, there's something queer about this place, so I think we ought to come back later on – probably tomorrow – and give it the once-over. Just a minute.' He climbed into the cockpit of the *Willie-Willie* and took his map from its pocket. Opening it flat on the ground, he studied it closely. 'This must be where we are,' he announced, pointing to the coast of East Prussia. 'This island here must be the island we're on – here's the strait – see? That gives us a line to Bergen Ait. Come on, let's get home.'

In a few minutes both machines were in the air, racing low over the uneasy water on a north-westerly course. The weather was still thick, but the clouds had lifted somewhat and were broken in many places, a condition which suited Biggles well, for although he flew through the open spaces, he kept close to the clouds, prepared to take cover in them should danger threaten.

However, they saw no craft of any sort, either in the air or on the sea, and twenty minutes' flying on full throttle brought them to within sight of their rocky home. The sea, while by no means as tranquil as they would have wished, had gone down considerably, and landing in the cove presented no great difficulty or danger.

Not a little satisfied at their safe return, Biggles taxied into the cave, calling loudly for Briny.

Instead, the Flight-Sergeant answered his hail.

'Where's Briny?' asked Biggles.

'He's gone, sir,' answered Flight-Sergeant Smyth.

'Gone? What do you mean – gone?'

'We thought you were down on the water somewhere. I told him you hadn't enough petrol to remain up all this time, so he took the launch and went to see if he could find you. I stood by here in case you returned.'

Biggles regarded the Flight-Sergeant seriously. 'Then heaven only knows what's happened to him,' he muttered. 'What time did he start?'

'It'd be just before lunchtime, sir.'

Biggles made a despairing gesture. 'Then *he* must have run out of petrol by this time. I expect he found the sea got too rough for him and had to run before the wind. Well, we can't do anything about it now,' he added after a glance at the mouth of the cave. 'It's nearly dark. We'll look for him in the morning – that is, if he doesn't come back during the night. You'd better look over these machines. We've lost the *Dingo*. By the way, before we left I told Roy to send a signal that we had got hold of the German naval code. Do you know if he sent it?'

'Yes, sir. The message was acknowledged.'

'Good.' Biggles turned to Ginger. 'You go and get some dry clothes on,' he ordered, 'then join us in the mess. It's about time we had something to eat.'

CHAPTER IX

What Happened to Algy

When at daybreak the following morning Biggles was informed that Briny had not returned he made immediate arrangements for a search. 'It's a nuisance because there are other things we should be doing,' he told Algy, for Ginger, tired out, had not awakened. 'We ought to explore that sandbank to see what the notice is about,' he continued. 'And there is a chance that we might overtake the *Leipzig* and plunk a mouldy[1] in her ribs. Further, I don't like this flying about in daylight; we are bound to be spotted sooner or later if we go on like this; the original idea was that we should only fly at night. However, while there's still a chance that Briny is drifting about in the boat we can't do other than try to find him. There's no need to wake Ginger. He can do with a rest. Two machines will be enough, anyway; there should always be one in reserve. I'll leave orders that Ginger is to stay where he is until we return.'

'We'd better go in different directions,' suggested Algy.

'More or less,' agreed Biggles. 'The gale came down from the north so the boat should be somewhere south of

---
[1] Naval slang for torpedo.

81

here. I'll cover the south-west. You take the south-east.' So that there could be no mistake, he marked the two sections lightly on his map with a pencil. 'If we find the boat, and it isn't too far away, we might try to tow it back – providing, of course, that the water is calm. Otherwise we shall just have to pick Briny up and abandon the boat. Come on, let's get off. I'm glad the weather is better, but it's getting late in the year and I wouldn't trust it too far. By the way, I've got Roy on decoding all the Boche messages that he has picked up; they may reveal something that needs our urgent attention so we'd better not be too long away.'

In a few minutes both machines – the *Willie-Willie* and the *Didgeree-du* – were in the air, heading away from the base on their respective courses. The sky was clear except for wind-torn streaks of cirrus cloud at a great altitude, but it was not long before the machines were out of sight of each other.

Algy, as arranged, continued to fly south-east, and, having climbed to 5,000 feet, settled down to study the surface of the ocean, which stretched away to the horizon, unbroken as far as he could see by a vessel of any sort.

For twenty minutes he cruised on, and then began turning in ever-widening circles, but no sign of the missing boat could he see. Far to the southward a dark grey line marked the position of the enemy coast, and for some time he kept away from it, for he was anxious to avoid being seen from the shore. But presently some floating wreckage attracted his attention, and in order to invest- igate it he had to approach nearer to the coast. He soon ascertained that the wreckage was not that of the motor- boat, and he was about to turn back towards the open sea when he perceived – what he had already suspected – that the land to the south was not the mainland, but the desolate sandbank on which they had landed the previous day.

Thinking the matter over, it struck him that it was by no means unlikely that Briny had been driven on to it, for the weather had come from the north, and as he knew from their visit that the sandbank was uninhabited, there seemed to be little or no danger in examining it more closely. With this object in view he began edging cautiously towards it, keeping as far out to sea as would permit a survey of the sandy beach.

He had followed it for perhaps three miles, and could see in the distance the bay in which they had landed, when a dark-coloured speck that could only be a human being detached itself from the dunes and ran down to the water's edge.

Algy could only fly nearer, for, from where he was, recognition was out of the question, but he felt that it was extremely unlikely that an enemy coastguard would expose himself in such a way, or behave in such a manner, for the figure was now gesticulating in a way that could only mean one thing. So he cut his engine and began to glide down; not with the intention of landing immediately, but in order to satisfy himself that the figure was actually that of the missing sailor. He felt pretty certain that it was, for he could not imagine who else it could be, but a doubt still lingered in his mind because there was no sign of the motorboat.

Gliding low over the solitary figure, he saw that it was, in fact, Briny, whose wild manifestations of joy reminded him in some curious way of Man Friday on Robinson Crusoe's island. A quick inspection of the shore satisfied him that it was safe to land, and in a few minutes the

Didgeree-du had run to a standstill on the beach not far from the stranded sailor.

Briny, grinning broadly, lost no time in reaching the aircraft. 'How did you know I was here, sir?' he inquired, saluting.

'I didn't,' Algy told him frankly. 'How did you get here, anyway? Where's the boat?'

'I don't know where the boat is and that's a fact, sir,' declared Briny. 'I swam here.'

'What do you mean – you *swam* here?'

'Well, sir, it was like this 'ere, sir. The gale caught me a beam, and pretty near swamped me. I couldn't make no 'eadway against it – although I remember once, off Cape Cod—'

'Never mind about Cape Cod. We're here. Where's the boat?'

'Well, as I was saying, sir, I 'ung on as long as I could. Then I ran out of petrol, and there I was, adrift as you might say. Then I see this place and thought I'd better get ashore. I couldn't get the boat in, so I 'ad to leave her and swim for it. I 'ad a job to get through the surf meself.'

'You must have nearly lost your life,' suggested Algy.

'I nearly lost me 'at,' returned Briny seriously.

'It would have been a pity to have done that,' muttered Algy sarcastically. 'What happened to the boat?'

'She drifted away after I got ashore. Then I ran up here as fast as I could.'

'Why run? What was all the hurry about?'

'Well, you see, sir, you wouldn't believe it, but I found meself right up against the German liner *Leipzig*. I knew her in a jiffy. I remember seeing her once, off Cape—'

'Just stick to the story. Where is the *Leipzig* now?'

84

'She's aground, sir, at the entrance to the channel, about four miles down the coast. I reckon she must have gone ashore in the dark at low water. Maybe they'll float her off when the tide turns. And there's something else here, too, although you wouldn't spot it if you didn't run slap into it, as I did, in a manner of speaking. There's a big shed round the next bend.'

'What sort of a shed?'

'A building as big as an aeroplane hangar, but not so high. It's painted all over with brown and yellow stripes. It stands on the edge of the water in as neat a little cove as you ever see.'

'What's in this shed?'

'I dunno, sir. It was dark when I was there. I lay down in the dunes nearby, reckoning to have a closer look when it got light, in case there was a dinghy in it. I was trying to find a way in when I see you coming, so I ran down on to the beach so as you'd spot me.'

'Did you find anything else on this bit of no-man's-land?'

'No, sir, that's the lot.'

Algy thought quickly. The absence of the motorboat was now explained, but he was more concerned about the shed Briny had described. That it was a secret supply depot seemed certain, and this, no doubt, accounted for the notice-board forbidding people to land. But Briny's description of the shed had been vague, and he felt that while he was there he ought to obtain more detailed information, for the Admiralty would be anxious to have full particulars. 'How far away is this shed?' he asked.

'About a mile, sir, I reckon.'

'And as far as you know there was no guard over it?'

'I didn't see a soul, sir.'

'In that case we'll go along and have a look at it. Get in.'

Briny started, 'Get in what, sir?'

'This aeroplane – what else do you think I mean? You can't see any motorcars about, can you?'

'What, me, sir?'

'Yes, you. Don't argue.'

'You don't mean you're going to *fly* there, sir?'

Algy wasted no more words. He bundled Briny into the back seat, and then, climbing in himself, taxied swiftly along the beach.

'Steady on, sir, me 'at's blowing off,' roared Briny, who was clutching at the sides of the cockpit.

Algy did not take off, for the short distance he had to travel made it unnecessary, and five minutes brought them to within sight of the building. He saw at once that Briny's description of it, as far as it went, was correct. The shed was a large but low structure, covering nearly half an acre of ground, built in a dip in the dunes at the landward extremity of a tiny cove so regular in shape that there was reason to suppose that it was artificial. The building stood at the very edge of the water; indeed, it was obvious that at high tide a boat of shallow draft would be able to moor up against the huge sliding doors; yet so cleverly camouflaged was it, in the same drab colours as the surrounding sand, that it would have been possible to fly over it at a low altitude without suspecting that it was there. It appeared to be absolutely deserted.

Seeing that it was impossible to taxi right up to the shed on the landward side on account of the dunes, Algy took the machine on to the water, and after raising his landing-wheels, made a cautious approach, prepared to take off the instant anyone appeared; but by this time he felt confident that had a guard been on duty he must have heard the approaching aircraft and revealed himself.

Nevertheless, he did not relax his caution as he taxied on, very slowly, until the *Didgeree-du* was alongside a wooden landing-stage that now appeared near the doors.

'Go and have a look round to make sure that nobody's about,' he told Briny. 'I'll stay here in case of accidents. If it's all clear I'll join you.'

Briny was soon back. 'Can't see a thing, sir,' he reported.

'What's in the shed?'

'I can't see, sir. There ain't no winders.'

'That's queer. You'd have thought there'd have been some sort of lighting.' Algy got out and tried the doors, but, as he expected, they were locked.

Meanwhile, Briny had climbed to the top of a dune, high enough to overlook the roof. 'There's skylights on top,' he announced.

'Skylights usually are on top, Briny,' smiled Algy. 'I'd better have a look. Give me a bunk up.'

Algy was soon on the roof which, like the rest of the building, was built of corrugated iron. Crawling to the skylight, he peered down through it. For a few seconds he could see nothing, for owing to the inadequate lighting the interior of the shed was in dim twilight. Presently, however, he was able to make out the broad details, enough to tell him that the shed was, in fact, a naval depot – for submarines, chiefly, he thought, judging by the torpedoes and a formidable stack of oil drums. Having seen enough for his immediate purpose he slid off the roof.

'It seems to be an ideal spot to plant a bomb,' he declared as they went back to the machine. 'And the sooner the better,' he added. 'If we can get rid of this lot, submarines coming here, relying on finding fuel, might find themselves stranded. I should say the sub, we sank was making for this place. Come on, let's get back; the C.O. ought to know about it.'

More than a little satisfied with the result of his survey, Algy turned the nose of the *Didgeree-du* to the mouth of the cove, and opening his throttle, roared away in the direction of the base.

So concerned was he with getting back that beyond keeping a watchful eye on the horizon for shipping he paid little attention to the sea below; so when Briny tapped him on the shoulder and pointed downwards, he followed the outstretched finger with a twinge of anxiety – anxiety that grew rapidly to acute alarm when his eyes found the object that Briny had spotted. Unquestionably, it was the wreckage of an aeroplane.

Cutting his engine, he side-slipped steeply towards it, and at a thousand feet his worst fears were realised, for showing just above the gently lapping waves was the circular red, white, and blue nationality mark of a British aircraft. For a moment he experienced a feeling of relief as he remembered that the *Dingo* had been lost, for he assumed, not unnaturally, that this must be the remains of it; but then he recalled that Ginger's machine had been burnt out, whereas there was no sign of fire on the wreckage.

As quickly as he dared he put the *Didgeree-du* down on the water and taxied up to the wreck. One glance was enough to tell him the worst. The machine was one of their own; and if further proof were needed, the boom-erang device on the crumpled fuselage, with the name *Willie-Willie* below, provided it. It was Biggles's machine.

And the reason for its present condition was apparent, for through fuselage and wings were the unmistakable gashes of shrapnel.

As white as death, Algy flung off his flying-coat and slid into the water, groping blindly for the cockpit. He found it. It was empty, as was the spare seat. Gasping, he returned to the surface, and climbed up on the nearest float of his own machine, from whence he stared at the wreckage as if he could not believe his eyes. His brain seemed paralysed. Biggles had been shot down. That was obvious. And judging from the number of hits registered on the plane, and the mangled condition of it, the crash must have been a terrible one. He tried not to believe it, but there was no getting away from the grim evidence before him.

It was Briny who discovered that the engine was missing. 'It looks as though it was chopped out with an 'atchet,' he declared in a sombre voice.

'Then that settles it,' returned Algy miserably. 'They shot him down and salvaged the engine for their own use. They would, of course.' He said no more. There was nothing else to say. Minutes passed and still he stood on the float, staring dumbly at the wreck. At last, realising that no good purpose could be served by remaining, yet hating to leave the spot, he climbed slowly into his cockpit. His eyes wandered over the surrounding sea.

Briny guessed what he was looking for. 'It ain't no use looking for the body,' he said gruffly. 'It 'ud sink. I remember—'

'We'll get back,' broke in Algy harshly, and taking off, he raced on full throttle for the base.

'Where's Mr. Hebblethwaite?' he asked the Flight-Sergeant, who came running along the catwalk to meet them.

'I don't know, sir,' was the unexpected reply. 'We haven't seen him for a couple of hours or more.'

'He didn't by any chance go with the C.O. after all?'

'No, sir. The C.O. hasn't come back yet.'

'I'm afraid he – won't be coming back,' said Algy slowly. He glanced at the *Platypus*, the spare machine, still riding at her mooring. 'Mr. Hebblethwaite must be about somewhere.'

'That's what we thought, sir, but we can't find him.'

Briny and the Flight-Sergeant watched in embarrassed silence as Algy unfastened the strap of his flying-cap and lit a cigarette. 'The war still goes on,' he said evenly. 'It can't stop because the C.O. is – missing. I am now in command here. Get my machine up to the derrick and sling a torpedo on it.'

'But are you going off again right away, sir?' asked the Flight-Sergeant.

'I am,' answered Algy curtly. 'You'd better make a thorough search for Mr. Hebblethwaite may have fallen and hurt himself. If he turns up tell him to stand by until I return. Those are my orders.'

The Flight-Sergeant saluted. 'Very good, sir.'

CHAPTER X

Ginger Goes Exploring

Had Ginger been aware of Algy's tragic discovery his state of mind would have been more harassed than it actually was – although he would have found it difficult to believe that possible.

He had been awakened by the roar of the two machines taking off to begin the search for Briny; he had guessed what they were going to do and hastily pulled on his slacks with the intention of confirming it. Outside he was met by the Flight-Sergeant, who gave him Biggles's order that he was to stand fast until the search party returned.

Annoyed with himself for having overslept, Ginger made his way back to his quarters, finished dressing, and had his breakfast. Thereafter he wandered about for the best part of an hour, killing time by examining the stores and visiting Roy in the signals room. Bored, he was on his way to the mess when it struck him that it was a good opportunity to explore the extremity of the cave – not so much for any particular reason as from idle curiosity. So fetching an electric torch from the stores, he started off over the loose rocks which began where the water ended. It struck him that he ought to have told the Flight-Sergeant where he was going, in case the machines returned before he did, but on second thoughts he concluded that this was unlikely, and proceeded on his way.

It is often fascinating, if futile, to speculate what might have happened if certain events had gone otherwise than they did, or to trace the tremendous consequences of incidents which, at the time, seemed of trivial importance. Thus it was with Ginger now. Had he returned and reported his proposed expedition to the Flight-Sergeant, the Flight-Sergeant would have known where he was; he in turn would have informed Algy, who, instead of taking off with a torpedo on board, would have first tried to locate him in order to tell him about his discovery of Biggles's machine. But Ginger did not return, and as he proceeded on over the rocks he would have been incredulous could he have foreseen the result of his failure to do so. It is certain that the history of 'Z' Squadron would have been altogether different from what it actually was.

He discovered, as he rather expected, that beyond the area of flat rock on which the depot was established the cave rapidly diminished in size, closing in on all sides until it was no more than a high, narrow tunnel, the floor of which was strewn with rocks worn round by centuries of erosion. He could not see why this should be, for the sea did not come as far, ending as it did in a rather slimy pool just beyond the depot. However, he assumed that exceptionally high spring tides penetrated farther into the island than they supposed, and made a mental note to warn Biggles of this, for it seemed not unlikely that at such times the floor of the depot would be inundated.

Thereafter the cave narrowed so rapidly that he was quite prepared for it to end abruptly at any moment; so confident was he that this was the case that he almost abandoned his survey, and it was only by the merest chance that he squeezed through a gap and turned the beam of the torch on what lay beyond. To his surprise he found that the cave, while not broadening to any great extent, became very high – so high, in fact, that the light of the torch failed to reach the ceiling.

The picture that now presented itself was in the nature of a gigantic crack, or fissure, the floor of which sloped upwards. Both the floor and walls of the cavity were polished smooth in a manner that suggested that water was responsible, and again this puzzled him not a little, for he could not imagine that the tide would rise so high. Wonderingly he took a few paces forward, and a clue to the mystery was provided when, stepping on something soft and looking to see what it was, the light of the torch revealed the decomposed carcass of a seagull.

On the face of it there was nothing remarkable about finding the body of a gull there, for there were legions of them on the outside of the rock, but his common sense refused to accept the obvious explanation – which was that the gull had made its way right up the cave in pitch darkness. Why should it? He had never seen a gull in the cave, or even one that looked like entering the cave, so why should this particular bird proceed up it so far and then perish miserably?

A few moments' reflection were sufficient to cause Ginger to reject the supposition that the gull had flown up the cave. Yet the gull was undoubtedly there. How had it got there? There could only be one answer to that question. There was another entrance to the cave; it was (he reasoned) through this other entrance that the water had entered, and since water does not run uphill, the other entrance must be higher than the one they habitually used. This at once presupposed that the gull had been carried to its present position by water flowing down through the rock.

Hunting about, Ginger soon found what he sought – a small pool in a depression in the floor. Dipping his fingers into it, he tasted it, and discovered that it was fresh, without any suggestion of salt. After that, deduction was fairly simple. Somewhere ahead, possibly on the top of the rock, there was a watershed through which rain water made its way down into the cave.

He went on now with renewed interest, for it seemed probable that he had found a way to the top of the rock; and if this was so it would serve a very useful purpose in that they would be able to command a much wider view of the ocean than had been possible from the mouth of the cave. So he pressed on, anxious to ascertain if this was really so.

The floor now began to rise steeply, strengthening his conviction that the fissure went to the top of the rock. It was tiring work, for not only was he travelling uphill, but he was often compelled to put the torch in his pocket to leave both hands free while he climbed a scree of loose shale, or an awkward-shaped boulder. However, he encountered no serious obstacle until he was brought to an abrupt halt by a face of overhanging rock some twelve feet high which completely blocked his path. Examining it closely, he suspected that he must be near the top, for a steady trickle of water flowed over the edge of the rock, which was worn to the smoothness of polished marble. It was covered with green slime, and to make matters more difficult, did not present a single foothold.

Disappointed at the thought of being thwarted just when success seemed assured, he sat down to get his breath and at the same time think out a way of overcoming the obstruction. He soon found one. There were plenty of pieces of loose rock lying about; these he proceeded to collect and pile one upon the other, forming a cairn, from the top of which he was able to reach the top of the obstruction. The rest was comparatively easy. Or so he thought.

How far he was wrong he discovered when, dragging himself up on the rock, his dangling legs struck the top of the hastily constructed cairn and sent it avalanching down the cave with a crash that brought his heart into his mouth, for until he realised what it was he had a horrible thought that the cave was collapsing on him. He perceived at once that this was going to make it very difficult for him to get down again. And it was only the first disaster, for as he was squirming over the edge of the rock, the torch, which he had put in his pocket, fell out, and went crashing down the way of the cairn.

Reviling himself for his carelessness, he dragged himself up and sat panting in utter darkness on the edge of the rock, thoroughly alarmed, wondering whether to go on or to try to get back, realising that the descent of the rock on which he was perched was not going to be easy. Even if he got down without hurting himself, and then found that the torch was broken – as seemed highly probable – his return was going to be a slow and tedious business. He remembered with relief that he had a box of matches in his pocket, but feeling in it with nervous haste, he discovered to his intense disappointment that there were only three matches in it.

He knew that, as he had already been away from the depot much longer than he originally intended, he ought to start back and leave further exploration for a future occasion, when he could begin more suitably equipped.

And he had, in fact, made up his mind to return forthwith when, happening to stare into the darkness ahead, he saw a grey streak not very far away, a patch of reflected daylight which could only mean that he was near the end of his journey.

In the circumstances it was only natural that he should begin walking towards it, feeling his way in order to conserve his precious matches. But he had only taken a few paces when he stepped into a void. Feeling himself falling, he made a terrific effort to preserve his balance; but it was too late, and the next instant, with an abruptly terminated cry of horror, he was splashing frantically in ice-cold water.

To fall into a pool of cold water at any time is bad enough, but to do so in utter darkness, in such a place as Ginger now found himself, was terrifying. Unable to touch bottom he had to swim, and instinctively struck out for the rock from which he had fallen, only to discover to his dismay that it was as smooth as a tombstone and the top was beyond his reach.

Had it not been for the one patch of grey light his plight would have been desperate indeed, and it was probably as much in order to escape the suffocating darkness as any other reason that he struck out towards it. To his unspeakable relief, after swimming a few strokes he found that he could touch bottom, so he staggered on through the water towards the blessed light, which, he felt, was the only thing that saved his sanity.

As he approached the spot it grew definitely lighter, and it was with a prayer of thankfulness that he finally dragged himself towards an aperture through which he could see what he had begun to wonder if he would ever see again – the blue sky. His haste to reach it was nearly his undoing, for he had forgotten all about his steep climb, and he was in the act of stepping forward when a spectacle so unexpected, and so alarming, met his eyes that a gasp of despair left his lips as he recoiled from it. The ground in front of him dropped sheer for a full four hundred feet. Indeed, it was even worse than that, for his precarious perch actually overhung the abyss, and he dropped on his knees in a spasm of vertigo as his eyes surveyed the dizzy height.

For a moment or two he remained still, fighting the weakness, angry that he should have succumbed to it. Then, taking himself in hand, he made a quick inspection of his position. He saw that instead of emerging on top of the rock as he had assumed would be the case, the fissure had ended some twenty feet below the top of the cliff, which he could now see above him. He perceived, too, that although this twenty feet of rock face was sheer, the surface was rough, and offered finger holds by which a skilled mountaineer might have made his way to the top; but he was not a skilled mountaineer, and the mere thought of trying to make the short but terrifying journey to the top made him feel physically sick.

Lying flat, he peeped furtively over the rim of his perch at the rocks far below, but they offered no clue to his whereabouts in relation to the cove. All he could see was a jumble of weed-covered rocks against which the waves – appearing from his height as insignificant as ripples – beat with measured regularity. Above them, minute white specks, which he knew were gulls, soared aimlessly. For the rest, the ocean stretched, an infinite expanse of dark green water, to a hazy horizon.

The next matter that engaged his attention was the source of the water that filled the subterranean lake, for he saw at once that it could not enter the aperture through which he had reached the light of day, so returning a few paces into the cave he examined the roof closely. It was his ears rather than his eyes that provided the solution, for a steady trickle of water told him that tiny invisible streams were percolating through flaws in the rock and finding their way into the natural reservoir, which, at the time of heavy rain, must overflow with the results already noted.

As there was nothing more to see Ginger now gave serious thought to his position. He became aware that he was cold, which was not surprising since he was soaked to the skin – his second wetting within a few hours. He was worried, too, about his long absence from the base, which he knew could not fail to cause alarm, and might upset Biggles's plans. He had dismissed all idea of trying to get to the top of the rock, so it was obvious that the only way he could return to the depot was by the path he had come up, although this now presented difficulties that appalled him.

In the first place it meant a swim across the lake, with no assurance that he would be able to find the fissure on the far side, or to climb up to it if he did find it. Assuming that he was successful so far, he was then faced with the disagreeable ordeal of dropping twelve feet in utter darkness on to a pile of boulders; for his matches, being wet, were now useless. He realised with an unpleasant twinge of fear that if he injured himself in the drop he was likely to die, in circumstances which he preferred not to contemplate. It is not surprising that the more he thought about things the less he liked the look of them, and sought desperately for an alternative.

Turning again towards the sea, it suddenly struck him that the watery sun might have sufficient power in it to dry his matches; if he could only get them dry, he thought, he ought to be able to transport them across the lake by tying them on his head. So with this object in view he took the box from his pocket and laid it, with the three matches beside it, in a sheltered pocket of rock reached by the sun. This done, he stood back prepared to await results. And he was still waiting, cold and uncomfortable, when a sound reached his ears that brought him round facing the sea, tense and expectant. It was the distant hum of an aero-engine; and presently he saw the plane, which he recognised at once for one of their own, heading straight towards the rock. What was more, he perceived that if it held on its present course it would pass fairly close to him. If only he could attract the pilot's attention – for he did not know who was flying the machine, and was unaware of Algy's tragic discovery – it would alter the whole position. Those at the base would then guess what had happened, and presently come to his assistance. Even if they failed to find the fissure, he would, by signalling to them as they flew over, be able to ask for the things he most needed – food, a rope, and a new torch.

Watching the machine, with fading hopes he soon realised that the chances of his being seen were remote. The pilot might glance at the top of the rock in passing, but he would hardly be likely to look closely at the face of the cliff, for there was no reason why he should. But if he, Ginger, could only reach the top, silhouetted against the skyline he could hardly escape being seen. Swiftly, he turned to make a closer inspection of the perilous passage.

Now that he had become accustomed to the dizzy height it did not look so formidable, and almost before he had made up his mind seriously to attempt it he found himself on the bottom ledge, groping with his fingers for a firm hold. Finding one, he shifted his feet, and clawed again for a fresh cleft for his fingers. And so he went on, not once daring to look down, but keeping his eyes on the rim above as it drew imperceptibly nearer.

Gasping with fear and exertion, his clutching fingers at last closed over it, and with a haste made desperate by the now close proximity of the aircraft, he dragged his aching body over the top and rolled clear of the edge.

In a moment he was on his feet, waving frantically. He was just in time to see the machine glide out of sight round a shoulder of the rock.

Sick with disappointment, he sank down, and cupping his chin in his hands, gazed disconsolately at the empty sea.

CHAPTER XI

What Happened to Biggles

When he took off to look for Briny, the only doubt in Biggles's mind, apart from a natural concern about the lost sailor, was that, by force of circumstances, they were doing much more daylight flying than he had ever intended, more than Colonel Raymond had intended, and without question more than was safe if the secret of the base was to be guarded. His natural caution told him that they could not hope to go on flying daily over hostile waters, at all hours, without sooner or later being observed, and the suspicions of the enemy being aroused. Already their activities must have attracted attention, he reflected, as he pursued his allotted course, climbing all the time to obtain a wider field of view.

For the best part of an hour, like Algy, he was unsuccessful, seeing no craft of any sort; and he was contemplating giving up the search when, far to the south, a minute object caught his eye. It was a vessel of some sort, but even at that distance he felt that it was too big to be the motorboat. Nevertheless, he decided to make sure, so he flew on, and presently perceived that the object was not one boat, but two, a fairly large one with a smaller one moored close to it.

A suspicion was already forming in his mind as he throttled back and began a long glide, in this way losing height to get a clearer picture of what was happening; and in a few minutes his suspicion was confirmed. The smaller of the two vessels was undoubtedly the missing motorboat; the larger one, as far as he could make out, appeared to be a trawler or drifter. Considering the situation, he came to the natural conclusion that Briny had been found adrift by the larger boat, which had – as it was bound to – offered assistance, either by taking it in tow or supplying it with fuel.

The question that now automatically arose in Biggles's mind was the nationality of the drifter. If it turned out to be a German ship, then he could do nothing about it, for while he was prepared to take chances, it did not occur to him to attempt such a fantastic undertaking as to try to capture the ship single handed. What concerned him far more was the fact that by this time he was being watched by the crew, who would lose no time in reporting his position.

Instinctively his eyes went to the drifter's stern to see if she was flying her nationality flag; and he saw that she was. What was more important, it was not the flag of the German Mercantile Marine. He was unable to identify it; all he knew was that it was not the German flag. And that was really all he cared about, for if it was not a German vessel it must belong to a neutral country, and since they were on the high seas he had nothing to fear.

Consequently, he continued the glide with the object of landing as close as he could to the two vessels, now lying hove to side by side. It may seem strange – and a few minutes later he was to reflect on this – that not for one single moment did it occur to him that the drifter might be flying false colours. So, with no suspicion his mind, he made a good landing and without hesitation taxied up to the larger craft. It is true that it struck him as odd that Briny was not in sight, but he came to the natural conclusion that he was in the captain's cabin going through unavoidable formalities, in which case there was a chance that he might not have heard the approaching aircraft.

Still without the slightest suspicion of anything wrong, Biggles taxied right up to the drifter; and if he had entertained any doubts the behaviour of the crew would certainly have dispelled them, for they were leaning over the rail, smiling with what he took for amiability. So he made the *Willie-Willie* fast, and stepping out on to a float, climbed aboard.

'Thanks for picking up my—' he began, but he got no farther. Instead he stared in amazement at what he now beheld. The members of the drifter's crew were still smiling, but from all sides he was covered by a whole range of weapons, from automatic pistols to a machine-gun.

Biggles knew that he had made a mistake, but he still did not understand entirely what had happened. His eyes went again to the flag still fluttering at the stern, thinking that he must have been in error in supposing it was that of a neutral country; but what he saw only confirmed his first impression, for the flag was that of a Scandinavian country, although he couldn't remember which. Further, the crew wore no uniforms except the blue jerseys commonly used by merchant sailors.

'What's all this about?' he inquired curtly, slowly looking round the circle of menacing weapons.

'You come this way,' ordered one of the men, who, in peaked cap and double-breasted reefer jacket, appeared to be one of the ship's officers. He beckoned towards the companion-way.

Unquestioningly Biggles followed. Indeed, he was in no case to argue. Further, he was anxious to get to the bottom of the apparent mystery as soon as possible.

Escorted by two men armed with rifles, he followed the officer down the steps and along a short corridor to a cabin, where he was disarmed and then searched, the contents of his pockets being taken away. There was a brief delay; then the officer returned and ordered Biggles to follow him. They went on a little way down the corridor and halted before a door that stood ajar.

'Come in, Major Bigglesworth,' said a suave voice, which Biggles recognised instantly.

A ghost of a smile flitted over his face as he pushed the door open, walked slowly across the threshold, and turned to face the man who was seated behind a small ship's desk. It was, as he already knew, his old enemy, Erich von Stalhein of the German Secret Service.

A curious expression, half cynical and half triumphant, was on the German's austere face; but his blue eyes were frosty.

Biggles considered him dispassionately. 'Congratulations,' he said.

'On what?'

'On changing your nationality. I can't recognise your new flag so I don't know what you've changed to, but since it couldn't be worse than it was when I last saw you, it must, perforce, be better. In the circumstances I can only congratulate you.'

A flush swept across von Stalhein's prominent cheekbones. 'Still as insolent as ever,' he said harshly.

Biggles helped himself to a cigarette from a box that stood on the desk and tapped it on the back of his hand. 'What have you done with my man – I mean, the fellow who was in the motorboat?'

'Ah! So there was only one.'

'You ought to know.'

'On the contrary, since the boat was empty when we found it we had no clue to the occupants or the number of them. We found the boat adrift – but we recognised its nationality, of course.'

Biggles looked into the German's eyes and thought he was speaking the truth – as indeed he was. 'The poor old fellow must have fallen overboard,' he said sadly.

'What was he doing in the boat?'

'Between ourselves, von Stalhein, he was looking for me. I was delayed on a flight yesterday and he came to the not unnatural conclusion that I had been forced down. When he, in turn, failed to return, I could hardly do other than look for him, could I?'

'Failed to return? Return where?'

'To the place where I expected to find him, of course.'

Von Stalhein leaned forward in his chair. 'Major Bigglesworth,' he said distinctly, 'I would advise you to be frank with me. We know you are operating somewhere near our coast. Where is your base?'

'How do you know I'm operating near your coast?'

'I will ask the questions if you don't mind. I repeat, where is your base?'

'Well, I suppose there's no harm in your asking,' murmured Biggles indifferently, 'but I have a higher regard for your intelligence than to suppose you expect a correct answer.'

Von Stalhein's thin lips parted for a moment in a frigid smile. 'From where did you take off this morning?'

Biggles made a deprecatory gesture. 'Oh, stop wasting time, von Stalhein. What is more to the point, I'm here, which should afford you considerable satisfaction. What are you going to do about it?'

'What do you expect me to do?'

'Hurry back home and tell the world how clever you are. Don't forget to mention that you borrowed a neutral flag, will you, because I shan't.'

'As it happens, I am too busy at the moment to do anything of the sort, but I will take steps to transfer you to a place where you will be safe pending your trial for espionage.'

Biggles raised his eyebrows. 'I suppose to one who doesn't mind sailing under a false flag, false charges are a mere detail.'

'Do you deny that you are a spy?'

'I most emphatically do. How can I be a spy when I am wearing a British officer's uniform? The rules of war demand that I be treated as a prisoner of war.'

'I am not concerned with the rules of war – or any other rules, Major Bigglesworth. You have given me far too much trouble in the past for me to run one single risk of your escaping. I've got you, and I'm going to keep you until I hand you over to those who will know how to deal with you – and if you have any optimistic views as to what that will be I advise you to dispel them. It so happens that my chief is not far away, so perhaps it would be as well to settle the matter immediately. With you disposed of I shall pursue my quest for your base with greater assurance.'

'I'll bet you will,' sneered Biggles.

'For the last time, I will offer you certain considerations in return for information concerning the position of your headquarters.'

'And for the last time, von Stalhein, nothing doing. Save your breath. You'll need it before I'm through with you.'

The German shook his head sadly. 'As you wish,' he said quietly. He gave a curt order to the escort and Biggles was marched from the room to a fairly comfortable cabin.

He heard a key turn in the door, and other sounds that told him that a guard had been posted.

Having nothing else to do, he sauntered to the porthole, not with any hope of getting through it for it was obviously much too small, but to see what happened to his machine.

Several men were working on it, cutting the engine from its bed. This was soon hoisted inboard, leaving the wrecked airframe floating on the water. The drifter then got under way, leaving the remains of the *Willie-Willie* rocking in its wake.

He was about to turn away when a gun crashed. For a moment he thought that the drifter was being attacked, but then he saw a shell burst near the derelict fuselage of his machine, looking strangely pathetic as it drifted alone on the water, and he guessed that von Stalhein had ordered it to be destroyed. That this supposition was correct was soon confirmed when several shots struck the machine, smashing the floats and causing it to settle slowly in the water.

Biggles turned away from the porthole. As far as he was concerned the *Willie-Willie* was a complete wreck; he gave it no more thought, nor did he look at it again, so he was unaware that the airframe did not entirely disappear, but remained awash, kept afloat by the air in the undamaged portions of the wings and elevators.

He was lying on his bed, smoking, turning his position over in his mind, when he was surprised to hear the drifter's engines slow down, and finally stop, while the clang of bells and shouted orders told him that something was happening. He knew that they could not yet have reached any of the German ports on the Baltic, for it was still twilight – about six o'clock as near as he could judge (his watch had been taken from him when he was searched), so he wondered what was happening. And it was with the object of trying to find out that he crossed again to the porthole. At first he could see nothing but water, but as the drifter slowly swung round he was astonished to see the hull of a big liner come into view. Nor was his surprise in any way diminished when he recognised it for the *Leipzig*.

What business the drifter had with the big ship he could not imagine, but he was soon to know. His door was unlocked. An escort appeared, and he was invited peremptorily to follow it. He had no alternative but to accept.

Across the deck of the drifter, up a gangway, and through a door in the side of the huge ship he was led, and finally halted outside the door of a stateroom. A brief delay, and in response to a sharp order he was marched inside.

He saw at once from the assembled company, and the manner in which it was disposed, that something in the nature of a court, or tribunal, had been convened; and he had no doubt as to the part he was to play. Facing him, seated at a long table, were four officers in German naval uniform. Between them sat an elderly man with iron-grey hair and piercing blue eyes who regarded the prisoner with more than passing interest. It was clear that he was the President of the court. At the end of the table sat von Stalhein, with some papers in front of him, and from one of these he now began to read so fast, in German, that Biggles had difficulty in following what was being said. However, he made no protest, for there was good reason to suppose that the result of the so-called trial was a foregone conclusion.

Von Stalhein finished reading and sat down. 'You understand?' said the President in English, looking at Biggles with frigid hostility.

'More or less,' returned Biggles, 'but before we go any farther I must protest against this court and the charges Hauptmann von Stalhein has enumerated. I am an officer of His Britannic Majesty's Forces, on active service, and under the rules of war I claim the privileges of a prisoner of war.'

The President smiled grimly, an unpleasant smile which told Biggles at once that his protest was a waste of time. He had expected as much, but still he had felt compelled to make it.

The President looked at the men seated on either side of him. 'I don't think we need waste any more time over this,' he said harshly in German. 'We have heard of this man Bigglesworth before; he is one of the best men in the British Intelligence Service, we have reason to know him, for he has given us a lot of trouble in the past.'

'A man dressed in the military uniform of his own country can hardly be called a spy, I think, if that is what you are trying to make out,' put in Biggles coldly.

'Pah! What is a mere uniform? Can you deny that since the outbreak of war you have been into Reich territory?'

'I don't deny it, but I was in the uniform I am now wearing. If that makes me a spy, then by the same token every German soldier in Poland is a spy, and the French troops in your country on the Western Front are also spies. Are they to stand trial for espionage if they are captured?'

'It is not the same thing,' said the President roughly, although he did not explain where the difference lay. 'You know, of course, the price a spy must pay when he is caught?' he added.

'Yes, of course I know,' replied Biggles bitterly.

The President nodded and made a note on a slip of paper. 'Then the sentence of this court is that you be shot to death in—' He broke off short, in a listening attitude. 'What's that?' he asked sharply.

Von Stalhein had jumped to his feet and hurried to a porthole. Simultaneously anti-aircraft and machine-guns broke into violent action. Above the din came the high-pitched scream of an aeroplane diving at terrific speed under full throttle.

Von Stalhein turned back swiftly into the room. 'You had better take cover, sir,' he said tersely. Then his eyes turned on Biggles, and his hand dropped to the revolver that he wore in a holster on his hip.

What he intended doing was not revealed, for at that moment the ship heeled over under the impact of an explosion so violent that everyone in the room was hurled off his feet. With it came a blinding sheet of flame, followed a split second later by swirling clouds of black, oily, high-explosive smoke.

CHAPTER XII

A Cold Swim

Biggles, coughing convulsively as the acrid fumes bit into his lungs, pushed aside a limp body that lay across him and staggered to his feet.. He tried to see what had happened, but the lights had gone out and the room was black with smoke which made his eyes smart unbearably; from the angle of the floor, though, he knew that the ship had taken a heavy list to starboard, a list that was rapidly becoming more pronounced. The air was filled with an appalling medley of sounds – shouts, the hiss of escaping steam, the vicious chatter of a machine-gun, a series of explosions deep down in the ship, and the gurgle of rushing water; somewhere not far away a man was groaning. A sickening smell of scorching mingled with the fumes.

Trying to beat the smoke away from his face with his hands, Biggles groped for the door; he found it, only to discover that it was jammed tight and half buried under collapsed girders. Clearly, there was no escape that way, so in desperation he turned to where he judged the nearest porthole to be. At the same time the smoke began to disperse somewhat, and through a grimy haze several things were revealed. The first thing he noticed was that it was nearly dark outside. Then he saw that a great jagged hole had been torn in the ship's side, and that owing to the list water was already pouring through it in an ever-increasing flood. Instinctively he made towards the hole, and looked out upon a fearful spectacle. He had seen much of war, but never anything on quite such a scale as this, and the deep twilight only served to make it more terrible. The water was full of debris of all sorts, among which at least a hundred men were swimming or splashing. Many were shouting, either from fear, or to make their position known to others. A splintered lifeboat hung vertically by its bows from a single davit, while over all lay a cloud of smoke and steam.

With the water now threatening to sweep him off his feet, Biggles turned back into the room to see what had become of the members of the court, not from mere curiosity, but with the deliberate object of helping any who were unable to help themselves, for it was obvious that it was only a matter of minutes before the stateroom would be submerged. He was only just in time, for in the deepening gloom he saw von Stalhein on his knees, taking aim at him with his revolver. Biggles sprang aside an instant before the weapon blazed, and the bullet ricocheted through the yawning hole in the ship's side.

Biggles snatched up a broken chair and flung it at the German. At the same time he shouted, 'Don't be a fool, man; let's get out of this. We can argue afterwards.'

Von Stalhein ducked and the chair missed its mark; but it served its purpose, for his next shot hit the ceiling.

Biggles waited for no more. It seemed to him that it was neither the time nor place for such a display of venom, so with a curt, 'All right; have it your own way,' he ran to the hole and dived into the sea.

For two or three minutes he put his entire energy into getting away from the ship; then, finding a piece of wreckage capable of supporting his weight, he rested, and took the opportunity of looking back. The sight that met his eyes remained engraved indelibly on his mind. The great liner was so far over on her side that her upper works still projected over his head. On its bulging side men were running about seemingly in an aimless fashion, although a few were jumping into the sea. He could no longer see the hole through which he had escaped – the hole which had wrought the havoc; but standing on a wrecked lifeboat he could see the lithe figure of von Stalhein, revolver in hand, looking out over the frothy water, apparently trying to see him.

'My goodness, how that fellow must hate me,' thought Biggles, for he could not imagine any normal-minded person behaving in such a way at such a time. 'Well, I suppose he can't help it,' he mused, and dismissed the German from his mind, for he had more urgent matters to attend to. He was still much too close to the ship for his liking, for he knew what a tremendous vortex would be created when it went down.

Aware that he would not be able to swim very far in his clothes, he proceeded to divest himself of everything except his vest and pants, and he had just completed this operation when he discovered that he had a companion. He recognised him for the officer who had been in charge of the escort when he had been marched before the tribunal. He saw, too, that he was in a bad way, so he asked him, 'What's the matter?'

'I can't see; the oil has got into my eyes,' was the answer.

Biggles pulled off his silk vest and thrust it into the man's hands. 'See what you can do with that,' he suggested.

Hanging on to the wreckage with his left hand, the man lost no time in following the advice. 'That's better,' he said presently. 'I seem to know your voice. Aren't you the Englishman?'

'That's me,' admitted Biggles cheerfully, as he began paddling the wreckage farther away from the sinking ship.

The man went on wiping his eyes, clearing them of the heavy oil which had clung to the lashes. 'Thanks,' he said, handing the vest back.

Biggles smiled and put it on again.

'Your fellow who did this made a good job of it,' declared the German.

'You're dead right; he certainly did,' agreed Biggles, spitting out a mouthful of sea water. 'What sort of aeroplane was it – did you see?'

'Yes, I saw it,' answered the sailor, and gave Biggles all the description he needed for him to realise that it must have been either Ginger or Algy who had dropped the torpedo.

'What were you doing round here, anyway?' was Biggles's next question.

'We were hove to at the mouth of the channel, waiting for the tide.'

'Channel?' The word made Biggles prick up his ears, for if it was the channel that separated the mainland from the sandbank on which he had landed with Algy and Ginger, then it gave him a rough idea of his bearings.

'How far are we from land?' he inquired, for it was now too dark to see anything.

'About a kilometre – more or less.'

'Which way does it lie?'

The man pointed. 'Over there. That's the German coast, but the sandbank on the other side is nearer, I think. If you're going to swim to it you'd better start.'

'Why – is there any hurry?'

The man was looking past Biggles at something beyond him, and turning to see what it was, Biggles saw the drifter, the existence of which he had completely forgotten. It was moving dead slow through the water picking up survivors; its boats had been lowered and were doing the same thing. He had no desire to be picked up, for he had a shrewd idea of what that would mean in the end – particularly after the sinking of the *Leipzig* by one of his machines. He preferred to take his chance on the sandbank, or even the mainland, where, if he was found, he might pass as a survivor of the ill-fated ship until he could make plans to escape. There was always a chance that he might be able to steal a small boat and get back to Bergen Ait.

'Thanks,' he told the German gratefully, and struck off into the darkness.

'*Lebewohl!* Good luck!' called the German after him.

For some time Biggles did not look back, but devoted himself to getting clear of the danger zone, the position of which he could judge roughly by the frequent hails of men still in the water as they tried to attract the attention of the rescuers. There was no moon, but in the light of the stars he could just make out the dark hull of the drifter. But of the *Leipzig* there was no sign. In a vague sort of way he wondered what had happened to von Stalhein, but he soon dismissed him from his mind, for the water was cold, and although he was a strong swimmer, he knew that if he did not soon reach land he might succumb to exposure. So settling down to a steady breast stroke, which he knew from experience he could keep up for a long time, he struck out in the direction in which, according to the sailor, the sandbank lay. At present he could not see it; not that he expected to, for it was too dark to see far. It was disconcerting, this swimming through the darkness towards an unseen objective, for should he miss it his position would be hopeless; at least, from what he had seen of the Baltic while flying over it, he would not have given much for his chance of being picked up by a ship.

An hour later he was still swimming, but not so strongly, for his body was fast becoming numb from the cold, and he dare not float to rest himself, as he could have done had the water been warmer. Shortly afterwards, however, he found it imperative to change his stroke, and in doing so he heard the sound which he had been hoping to hear – the measured beat of surf on the sandy shore.

With a prayer of thankfulness he struck out with renewed vigour, and a few minutes later found him staggering through shallow water to the beach. Not until he had crawled up on the sand did he realise how far he was spent; but even then what he feared most was that he might collapse from cold, for the night air was chilly. So with the object of restoring his circulation by the only means available, he set off at a jog-trot along the lonely beach, which seemed to stretch to infinity in front of him. He was deadly tired, but still he ran on, deriving some comfort from the warmth that his exercise was producing.

How far he ran he did not know. Nor did he care. He only knew that he seemed to have been running for hours when just ahead he observed some fairly high sand-dunes, and towards these he directed his steps, hoping to find shelter where he could take a breather. Breaking into a sprint to satisfy himself that he still had it in him, he dashed round the foot of the first dune, and collided with stunning force with somebody coming the other way.

Tired as he was he was unable to keep his balance, and after a final stumble, in which he caught a glimpse of a dark human form, he plunged headlong into the loose sand.

Quick as he was getting on his feet, the other was quicker, and he went over backwards again with a gloved hand pressed savagely over his mouth. Gripping his assailant with his hands, and doubling his knees under him, he endeavoured to fling him off, but only succeeded in causing them both to roll over and over down the sloping sand. They arrived at the bottom with Biggles underneath. He saw an arm raised to strike. The butt end of a revolver showed for an instant against the sky, and he clutched at it desperately. His assailant sought to free his arm, but just as furiously Biggles held on to it. Then came the end. But it was not the end Biggles expected, for, the struggle coming on top of his previous exertions, he was on the point of collapse.

It came when his opponent suddenly shouted, 'Hi! Briny! Help!'

'Algy,' gasped Biggles weakly. 'Get off my chest, you maniac!'

CHAPTER XIII

An Alarming Discovery

The pressure on Biggles's chest relaxed with amazing promptitude.

Algy was incapable of speech, and for a while he could only yammer foolishly. 'What are you doing here?' he managed to get out at last.

Biggles lay flat on his back, panting heavily. 'What do you think? Making sandcastles with my little spade and bucket? What are you playing at, anyway?'

'Oh, I'm just collecting pretty pebbles for the kids to play marbles with,' replied Algy. 'As a matter of fact, I'm on my way to blow up the dump.'

'Dump? What dump?'

'Ah! Of course, I forgot, you don't know about that. Briny found a dump.'

'Briny? Where is Briny? What's he been doing? Am I going crazy or are you? You talk as if he'd found a dump kicking about on the beach.'

As if in answer to the questions, Briny himself charged round the dune, swinging a rifle in a most dangerous manner.

'Be careful what you're doing with that thing, you fool,' snapped Biggles irritably, for what with shock and fatigue he was in no mood to be polite.

Briny stopped with ludicrous suddenness, the rifle poised. Then, slowly, it dropped to the ground. 'Luv a duck, sir, if it ain't the C.O.,' he gasped. 'What have you been doing, sir, if I may make so free as to ask?'

'Riding round the front in a hansom cab with Hitler,' grated Biggles with bitter sarcasm. 'It's time we stopped asking fool questions and got this thing straightened out,' he added with a change of tone. 'I'll start. I found the motorboat, but was captured by von Stalhein in a drifter and arrived on the *Leipzig* just as somebody was thoughtful enough to sling a mouldy in her ribs. I jumped into the sea and swam here. That's all.'

'I slung the mouldy,' admitted Algy.

'Thanks. You'll never sling a better one as long as you live,' declared Biggles. 'I'll tell you why later on.'

'I found Briny stranded on this sandbank,' explained Algy. 'On the way back to the base we found the remains of your machine, so thinking you were a goner I went mad dog. I had a crack at the *Leipzig* first. Then I went home for a time-bomb. Oh, I forgot to say that when I picked up Briny here we found a dump – a sort of Hun naval store. We were going to blow it up when I ran into you. I brought Briny along to guard the machine while I did the dirty work.'

'I see. That explains things,' said Biggles, rising stiffly to his feet. 'Somebody will have to lend me a jacket. I'm cold. I've been swimming for an hour or more in this perishing ditch.'

Briny took off the flying jacket he was wearing and passed it over. 'I remember once—' he began.

'Then forget it,' cut in Biggles, putting on the coat. 'And now, if somebody would be kind enough to take me home, I should like to warm my tootsies by the stove.'

'What about the dump?' asked Algy. 'I've got the time-bomb here.'

'You can stick it in a crab hole or play hop-scotch with it for all I care. I don't feel like fooling about any dumps, and I've heard all the explosions I want for one day. Let's get back. I'll send Ginger to attend to the dump.'

'You won't,' replied Algy promptly.

'Why not?'

'He's missing.'

'Missing! Since when?'

'Nobody's seen him since we took off early this morning.'

'Is the spare machine still in the cave?'

'Yes.'

'Then he must be on the island somewhere. Suffering Mike! What sort of a squadron have I got? What does the young ass think he's at – a picnic?'

'When you find him you can ask him.'

Biggles thought for a moment. He was not seriously upset about Ginger, for if the *Platypus* was still at its moorings it was obvious that he could not be far away, for the simple reason that he had no means of leaving the base. It struck him, however, that if the dump was to be destroyed, now was the time to do it, for it seemed certain that the Germans would cause a search to be made for him, and the sandbank, being the land nearest to where the *Leipzig* was sunk, would be one of the first places they would look at. He decided, therefore, that if anything was to be done about the dump, now was the best time, for to return later might result in an encounter with a search party sent out to look for him. Indeed, he was only too well aware of how dangerous their whole project had already become. It was, in fact, precarious, now that von Stalhein knew they were operating in the district – assuming that he had survived the *Leipzig* disaster. He knew the German well enough to know that, actuated as he was by personal motives as well as those of patriotism, he would not rest until he had located their base; and it could be only a question of time before he examined Bergen Ait. The fact that the islet was supposed to be the property of a neutral state would weigh little with a man as thorough and relentless as Erich von Stalhein. However, he refrained from depressing the others by communicating to them these disconcerting thoughts.

'All right,' he said at last, 'I'll tell you what we'll do. For the three of us to try to squeeze into the machine is going to be a difficult business, particularly as I'm not dressed for what you might call skylarking. Algy, suppose you take Briny home and then come straight back bringing my spare kit with you. You ought to make the round trip inside an hour. I'll get everything ready here for the big bang the moment you return. That seems to be the easiest way.'

'As you say,' agreed Algy.

'Where is the dump?'

Algy pointed. 'About half a mile along the beach.'

'I see. To save our legs you might as well land a bit nearer to it when you come back. By the way, what exactly does this dump consist of?'

Algy described what he had seen.

Biggles's eyes opened wide. 'It sounds to me as if there ought to be some stuff there that we could use ourselves. I mean, we might find ourselves out of petrol one day, in which case we should be glad to have a reserve supply. Before blowing the place up I certainly think we ought to have a closer look at what it contains.'

Algy nodded. 'I didn't think of that. But you can't get into it. It's locked up.'

'You say it's made of corrugated iron?'

'That's right.'

'Then with a drill and a hacksaw we ought to have no difficulty in cutting a hole through the side. We may as well try it, anyway. You bring the tools back with you. Bring a torch and anything you think might be useful. If we find the job of getting in is too much for us we'll give it up and blow the place sky high as you originally intended. But we mustn't stand here talking any longer. You get off and get back as quickly as you can.'

Algy thought the plan was a sound one, so after settling a few minor details, he returned to the machine, taking Briny with him.

Biggles was left alone on the sandbank. As soon as he heard the machine take off, he picked up the time-bomb, which was still lying where it had fallen when the collision had knocked it out of Algy's hand, and started off towards the dump. The moon was now creeping up over the horizon, so it did not take him long to find the shed and the adjacent moorings, which he examined with considerable interest. He then went round to the rear wall, where he arranged the bomb, for he thought it would be as efficient there as anywhere if it were decided to use it. After that, as there was nothing more he could do, he began making a closer inspection of the building.

He did not learn much, however, for he soon discovered what Algy already knew – that there were no windows. He suspected that there were skylights, but he had no means of getting on the roof – not that he made any serious attempt to do so, realising that the interior would be in utter darkness.

Having nothing to do now but wait, it was with profound satisfaction that he heard the hum of Algy's engine, really before he expected him. He walked briskly towards the sea, and by the time Algy had landed, and taxied into a sheltered creek about two hundred yards away, he had joined him.

Algy tossed him a vacuum flask. 'Take a swig of that,' he said. 'It's hot coffee – it should warm you up. Here's your kit,' he added, throwing a bundle after the flask.

Biggles began getting into his clothes as quickly as he could, from time to time taking gulps of coffee with grateful relish. 'Is Ginger back yet?' he inquired.

'No.'

Biggles paused for a moment in what he was doing. 'I don't like the sound of that,' he said slowly. 'He wouldn't stay away all this time if he could get back. I'm afraid he's met with an accident.'

'Briny and the Flight-Sergeant have hunted high and low for him – in fact, they're still looking.'

Biggles resumed his dressing. 'This squadron of mine doesn't seem to be living up to its name,' he said bitterly. 'There hasn't been much boomeranging about it lately. Apart from losing two of our machines, we seem to have gone out of our way to scatter ourselves all over the blinking Baltic. We'd better not waste too much time here. Did you bring the tools?'

Algy, who had climbed down from the machine, held them up. 'I've got a length of line in my pocket, too, in case we have to get down through the skylight.'

'Good!' said Biggles, putting on his flying-coat. 'Let's go and rip the hide off this tin toy-shop of Mister Hitler's.'

They were soon at work, choosing the rear wall, with a good deal more noise than Biggles liked, but making such good progress that in half an hour, by levering up the piece they had cut, they were able to crawl through into the interior of the building.

Biggles flashed the torch around as Algy got through behind him. 'Shades of Guy Fawkes!' he ejaculated. 'What a collection. We really ought to save this little lot for firework day.'

He began walking round, turning the light of the torch on bombs, torpedoes, shells, machine-guns, sub-machine-guns, and every conceivable form of ammunition. But what interested him more than these were the fuel tanks, and the carefully labelled collection of spare parts and accessories for all sorts of marine craft. With the painstaking thoroughness of a reconnaissance pilot, he made a mental note of everything he saw as they walked on slowly through the corridors. He pointed to a steel airscrew. 'Aircraft evidently use this place as well as submarines and destroyers,' he said. 'I don't know what to do about it, and that's a fact. It might do us a bit of good one day if we left the stuff here; on the other hand, it might do the enemy a lot more harm if we destroyed it. I've a good mind to radio Colonel Raymond and ask him for instructions. He ought to know about it, anyway. I—'

He broke off suddenly, in a tense attitude. The light went out as he switched it off, leaving them in darkness.

'It sounds as if somebody has found my machine,' said Algy in a low voice, for there was no mistaking the sound that had alarmed them. It was an aero-engine.

'It isn't your machine. There's more than one,' returned Biggles in a hard voice. 'It sounds to me like a formation – flying low, too.'

'They're coming this way,' declared Algy a moment later.

Biggles was still listening intently. 'I don't think it's a formation after all,' he said slowly. 'I should say it's a big multi-engined job.'

As he spoke the roar of the engines died away, but they could still hear the wail of wind through wires.

'It would be a joke if it was coming here, wouldn't it?' murmured Algy.

'It might be your idea of a joke, but not mine,' replied Biggles curtly. 'When I first saw the Baltic I thought it was a pretty deserted place, but lately it seems to be swarming with vehicles of one sort and another. That machine's coming a lot too close for my liking. We'd better get outside.'

'I hope they don't spot my machine.'

'I shouldn't think there's much chance of that in this light. Come on, let's get outside. I daren't use the torch; they'd spot it through the skylight; mind you don't knock your eye out on the blunt end of a crankshaft. Keep close to me. I think I can find my way to the hole.' So saying, Biggles began groping his way towards the spot where they had affected an entrance.

Some time before they reached it, it became obvious that even if the aircraft did not actually intend landing, the pilot was gliding down to survey the spot, for the metal building vibrated with noise. Consequently, it was with more haste than dignity that they scrambled through the hole and stared up into the starlit heavens.

They were not long finding the aircraft – for, as Biggles had surmised, it was a single machine.

With its navigation and cabin lights ablaze, a four-engined flying-boat was turning with the majestic deliberation of a battleship towards the anchorage that adjoined the shed.

'It *would* decide to arrive at this moment, wouldn't it?' said Biggles savagely, as he forced down the jagged metal flap which they had raised to get inside the building. 'Look out! Get down!'

He flung himself flat, his body pressed close against the corrugated iron, as a parachute flare burst a hundred feet over their heads and flooded the scene with dazzling white light. And thus they were compelled to remain until the keel of the giant flying-boat kissed the water, and surged on towards the wide double doors of the supply depot.

The instant the light exhausted itself Biggles was on his feet. He started to move forward, but pulled up short. 'Where's the time-bomb?' he said tersely. 'I put it down here.'

'I took it inside with me. I thought if we used it, it would make a better job of things there.'

Biggles muttered something under his breath. 'I suppose you acted for the best,' he conceded, 'but we daren't go in there now to fetch it. I doubt if we could find it, anyway, without a light. If they come across it there'll be a fine old hullaballoo. We'd better get back to your machine ready for a snappy take-off.'

By this time the huge aircraft had taxied right up to the building. Its propellers stopped as the pilot switched off the ignition, and it was obvious that the crew were about to come ashore. Its lights reflected on the water, and the sound of voices came clearly through the still night air.

Biggles caught Algy by the arm, and together they ran to the nearest sand-dune, from where they made their way quickly to the place where they had left the *Didgeree-du*. There was no particular need for caution, for they knew that their presence was unsuspected, and it was natural to suppose that the German airmen were too taken up with the task of mooring their machine to worry about anything else.

Biggles doubled round the last dune, and saw the soft gleam of the *Didgeree-du*'s wings. 'Here she is,' he said quickly, and then, as the entire machine came into view, pulled up dead. 'Good heavens! That's done it,' he cried aghast.

Algy joined him. There was no need to ask what had happened: it was too painfully obvious. The incoming tide had flooded the creek to a depth that could be estimated roughly by the fact that gentle waves were lapping against the bottom of the fuselage. The floats were under water, and the machine, for some reason not immediately apparent, had sunk over to one side. Water was still pouring into the creek, turning it into an ever-widening lake.

For perhaps a minute Algy could only stare at the scene as the enormity of the disaster slowly penetrated into his brain. 'I don't understand this,' he muttered. 'Why doesn't she float?'

'Because her wheels have sunk into the sand, that's why,' answered Biggles grimly.

CHAPTER XIV

Von Stalhein Again

For the best part of an hour they strove desperately to drag the *Didgeree-du* from the sand that clung tenaciously to her wheels, but in vain, and Biggles reluctantly gave his opinion that they were wasting their time.

'She's fixed as tight as a limpet on a rock,' he announced disgustedly. 'We shall have to wait for the tide to go down and then dig her out. It must be nearly high water now – I suppose that's why the flying-boat came here just at this time. We can't afford to lose the machine. I should look a pretty fool having to report to Raymond that we were down to a single aircraft.' Biggles sat down on the sloping side of a dune and regarded the *Didgeree-du* with disfavour.

'Waiting for low tide is all right as long as these chaps push off before daylight,' remarked Algy. 'As a matter of fact I doubt if it will be right out before dawn. If the Boche take off in daylight they'll spot the machine for a certainty. D'you suppose they're going to fly calmly round and watch us dig it out? Not likely. They'd shoot us up – or send a radio signal saying that we were here.'

'You're becoming a perishing pessimist.'

'It's no use blinking at facts.'

'All right. Well, there's no sense in sitting here just staring at the blinking thing.'

'What do you suggest we do then – start a sing-song or something?'

'We might creep up to the shed and try to hear what the Boche are talking about. I mean, we might learn how long they propose to stay here. What are they up to, anyway?'

'Refuelling, I expect – unless, of course, they've landed here to make mud-pies,' sneered Algy sarcastically.

'You talk as if you'd had a rush of mud to the brain,' declared Biggles with asperity as he got up and began moving towards the shed, taking care to keep behind the dunes.

Algy followed him, and in a few minutes they were within sight of the building and the big flying-boat.

'They've put the cabin lights out,' observed Biggles. 'If that's anything to go by, they've no intention of moving before daybreak.'

'It looks that way to me,' agreed Algy. 'Judging by the casual way that fellow is coiling up the hosepipe, they're going to stay here for the duration.'

They did not attempt to approach the door, for an occasional figure passed in and out, but from where they were they could see that the big sliding doors had not been opened; instead, a small door let into the larger one – an arrangement frequently used in such buildings – was being used. As there was nothing more to be seen from the position they now occupied they made a cautious advance to the hole in the rear of the building. Biggles had closed it when they had made their precipitate retreat, but it was only the work of a minute to lever it open again. They knew before they did so that some form of illumination had been turned on inside, for a shaft of yellow light poured through the open door, so they were not surprised to find that two large arc lamps, with shades to throw the light downwards, made the interior as bright as day. They could hear people moving about, and – a homely sound – the rattle of crockery; there was also a low buzz of conversation, but they could see no one on account of the high piles of stores that interrupted their view. What they could see, however, was the time-bomb, resting on the floor a few feet away.

'I'm going in to retrieve that bomb; we may need it,' whispered Biggles. 'I'll try to find out what they're up to at the same time. Stay where you are.'

There appeared to be no particular danger in fetching the bomb, for, by bending low, Biggles could keep under cover. Having reached it, he rose furtively and peeped over the top of a stack of shells. The sight that met his eyes brought a smile to his lips, it was so human. Some distance away, perhaps a matter of thirty paces, some boards had been put across two piles of stores, forming a table. Round this were seated seven men, all young, still wearing their flying kit, but with jackets thrown open and helmets on the backs of their heads. They appeared to be in the best of spirits, as they had reason to be, for steaming plates on the table told their own story.

Not until then did Biggles realise how famished he was, and an insane desire to join the party came over him. He dismissed it reluctantly and tried to catch some words of the conversation, but as far as he could make out the men were not talking about their work at all, but – another human touch – were chuckling over a recital of the war rumours then circulating in Berlin.

Biggles remained where he was for some time, but then, as there was no indication that the conversation would turn to more relevant topics, he went back to Algy.

'I can't hear much, but from their manner I should say they're going to stay here for some time,' he announced. 'At the moment they're having a lovely picnic.'

'Then what about shooting 'em up and having a basinful of soup ourselves?' suggested Algy, ever practical.

'It may sound silly, but that'd be a bit too much like murder for my liking. I've a better idea than that.'

'What is it?'

'I've got a feeling that I'd like to borrow their big boat.'

'And abandon the *Didgeree-du*? Not likely.'

'We could come back and fetch it later on.'

'But they would find it.'

'Not necessarily. Anyway, if we covered it with mud and rushes there's a chance they wouldn't tumble on it. They'll stick around the shed. My feeling is, if we can get hold of that boat we ought not to let the opportunity pass. The *Didgeree-du* may be bogged permanently for all we know, and if that turned out to be the case we should be in a fine old mess.'

'You're right there,' admitted Algy. 'All right then; let's have a dekko at the front of the building and see what's happening there.'

'There's no need for us both to go. You get back to the machine and start camouflaging it while I do the reconnoitring. I'll join you as soon as I can.'

Without protest Algy disappeared into the dunes. Biggles, taking the time-bomb with him, made his way to the front of the hangar, where he found his task even easier than he expected, for the place was deserted, and the great boat rode silently at her moorings, made fast by a single line from the bows. He scrutinised the shadows closely for a sentry, but he could not see one – not that he expected to, for had he been in the position of the chief pilot of the flying-boat he would not have thought it necessary to mount a guard.

Turning his attention to the door, a broad smile spread over his face as he realised how completely chance had played into his hands; for the small door had not only been left open, but there, on the outside, was the key still in the lock. He waited for no more, but hurried back to Algy, whom he found just completing his task, made possible by the fact that the tide was now receding, and the creek was only inundated to a depth of two feet or so. It was now possible to see how hopelessly the *Didgeree-du* was bogged, for her wheels, one lower than the other, were completely under the sand.

Biggles wasted no time in idle contemplation of it. 'Come on,' he said urgently. 'We're all set. The machine's as good as ours.' Briefly he related the circumstances. 'Lend me your pencil, and let me have a page out of your notebook,' he concluded.

'What's the idea?' inquired Algy as he passed them over.

'I'm going to slip a note under the door telling those fellows about the hole in the wall.'

'Why?'

'Otherwise they may never find it.'

'What does it matter?'

'We can't leave the poor blighters to starve to death – anyway, they may be some time getting out, and I'm going to drop an egg on this place at the first opportunity. I should hate to do it thinking they might still be inside. Bombing's all right up to a point, but—'

Algy nodded. 'Yes, to bomb the place after pinching their boat would be adding insult to injury,' he agreed. 'Well, let's get on with it.'

They returned to the store depot, where they found everything just as Biggles had last seen it. 'You get to the boat and make ready to cast off when you see me coming,' he ordered. 'The engines must still be warm, so they ought to start at the first spark.'

He gave Algy time to reach the boat, and a few minutes' grace after he had gone aboard, and then crept silently to the door. Very gently he closed it. The key turned in the lock without a sound. Then, taking the note he had written from his pocket, he slipped it through the crack. He could still hear the murmur of conversation inside; it had gone on, unbroken, all the time he had been near the door, and he knew that the Germans were in blissful ignorance of what was happening. Picking up the time-bomb, more because they had only one or two at the base and he thought they might need it, than for any immediate purpose, he walked down to the flying-boat and went aboard.

'It's all right, you can relax; there's no hurry,' he told Algy, who had cast off and was now sitting with his hand on the throttle.

'Shall I start up?' asked Algy.

'Go ahead.'

'Are you going to fly her or shall I?'

'You,' returned Biggles briefly. 'I'm going to have a nap. Tell me when we're home.'

With his left hand on the master throttle, Algy started the engines, and the giant boat began to surge towards the open sea.

Biggles opened a side window and looked out, but nothing happened, for reasons which he knew. Still, he smiled at the thought of the consternation that must now be going on within the tin walls of the building.

The flying-boat rocked gently as she struck the swell of the Baltic; then her engines picked her up and she roared into the night sky.

Biggles noticed that Algy was laughing. 'Yes, war's a funny thing,' he remarked, supposing that he knew the cause of Algy's mirth.

'It's funnier than you think,' declared Algy, going off into fresh peals of laughter.

Biggles looked at him curiously. 'Why this sudden flood of hilarity?' he demanded. 'Come on, what's the joke?'

'Did you ever read in the Bible about a camel going through the eye of a needle?'

Biggles stared. 'I don't get it.'

'I'm only wondering what we're going to do with this leviathan when we *do* get her home.'

Biggles frowned suddenly as understanding flashed upon him. 'Stiffen the crows,' he muttered, 'I hadn't thought of that.'

'Neither had I, until we started. She won't go into the cave, or anything like it. Even if we were able to pull her wings off, which I doubt, the fuselage would just about block the entrance.'

Biggles stroked his chin. 'It's just like you to think of something difficult when everything looked easy,' he observed bitterly. 'Work it out yourself. I'm tired. Tell me when we get to the island. I'm going to sleep.'

And sleep he did, until Algy nudged him in the ribs and warned him that they were nearly in.

Biggles woke up and stretched, yawning. 'That's better,' he announced as the flying-boat glided down to a smooth landing, with enough way on her to carry her to the mouth of the cave. Opening a side window he looked out, ready to hail if he saw anyone, for he realised that there was a chance of their being fired on. But the base seemed to be entirely deserted.

'Where the deuce is everybody?' asked Algy.

'I expect they're asleep,' returned Biggles. 'Don't make a noise, there's no need to wake them up,' he went on, as they walked along the huge, tapering wing of the flying-boat and jumped ashore.

'Hm, this is odd,' he continued a few minutes later as they reached the depot, still without anyone appearing. 'One would have thought there would have been some-body on duty.'

They went all round the depot, but the only person they could find was Roy, who, with earphones still clamped on his head, lay asprawl his desk, sleeping the sleep of exhaustion. The British and German code-books lay beside him; the pencil with which he had been working was still between his fingers.

'Poor little beggar,' whispered Biggles, 'he's absolutely all in, which isn't surprising considering the length of time he's been at this desk. I suppose he tried to hang on until we got back, but flopped out over his work. You can't keep awake indefinitely. I've been asleep at the joystick before today. I think we may as well let him sleep on. Ginger isn't back, that's certain, but what on earth can have happened to Briny and the Flight-Sergeant.'

'I suppose they've gone to look for Ginger.'

'Yes – of course, that's it. Well, I must say this looks a pretty dead sort of hole. Hullo! What's this?' Biggles picked up a sheet of paper that lay by itself half concealed under Roy's face. Very gently he drew it clear and picked it up. It was marked across the top, in big block letters, URGENT. 'Good heavens, it's a signal,' he said tersely. 'It must have come in while we were away. Roy's decoded it, too – what's this—?'

Biggles read the message aloud. '"Urgent. Enemy naval supply depot suspected on north-east coast of East Prussia, probably among sand-dunes north of the Gutte Channel. It is of vital importance that it be located immediately and destroyed."'

Biggles stared at Algy. 'What do you know about that?' he muttered.

'It must be the place we've just left.'

'Of course it is. There couldn't be two of them so close to each other. What a confounded nuisance we didn't finish the job while we were there. Well, it'll have to wait now. I'm dead on my feet. I couldn't take a machine to that sandbank and back if the Empire depended on it. I can hardly see out of my eyes.'

'You look about played out,' murmured Algy seriously. 'You're certainly not fit to fly until you've had some sleep; you'd only crash and kill yourself if you tried. I tell you what: I'm fresher than you are, you lie down and get some sleep. I'll take the *Platypus* and make a quick trip to the sand-bank. I hope those fellows are not still inside the building.'

Biggles glanced towards the entrance of the cave and saw that it was now grey with the approach of dawn. 'They'll be outside by now,' he said definitely. 'They will have found my note telling them how to get out, so they'll probably be on the beach watching for a ship to take them off. When they see you coming they'll guess what you're going to do and clear off. If they hang around it'll be their own funeral. After all, there's a war on and orders are orders. All right, old lad. I'd be obliged if you would slip back and do the job; one bomb ought to be enough.'

'I'll get along right away,' declared Algy. 'You get some sleep. When I come back we'll hunt round for the others.'

'Good! I'll see you off.'

Without waking Roy, they left the signals room and made their way along the catwalk to the *Platypus*. A single 112lb, bomb was slung on the central bomb-rack, and Algy was about to get into his seat when Biggles picked up the time-bomb which he had brought back with him. 'You might as well take this,' he suggested. 'If you miss with your bomb, and the Boche are a fair distance away, you might land and do the job with this one. We've got to make sure of the place. It won't take up any room, anyway, so no harm will be done if you have to bring it back.' He placed the square charge of explosive on the rear seat.

'I tell you what would be a good thing to take,' said Algy suddenly.

'What?'

'One of those sub-machine-guns from store. If the Huns are still about, and I expect they will be, they might start shooting at me, and – well, I'd feel happier if I had a mobile weapon in case I had to land, or was forced down.'

'That's true,' agreed Biggles. 'Stand fast. I'll fetch you one.'

He was soon back with a vicious-looking weapon, and some clips of ammunition, which he arranged securely within Algy's reach. 'Don't forget this is our last machine,' he reminded him as Algy climbed into the cockpit.

'I'll try not to bust it,' Algy promised.

Biggles ran to the mouth of the cave and looked up at the sky. 'Don't be too long away,' he called. 'I don't like the look of the weather.'

Algy waved to signify that he had heard and taxied out on to the cove.

Biggles waited for him to take off and then made his way slowly to the mess. He looked into the kitchen as he passed, wishing that he had the energy to get himself some breakfast; but his one overwhelming desire was for sleep, and he lay back on his bed with a sigh of relief, not intending to sleep immediately, but to rest for a few minutes before undressing. But nature, long denied, decided otherwise. His eyes closed, and he sank into a heavy dreamless sleep of utter weariness.

The hour hand of the clock on the mantelpiece ticked its way slowly round the dial, and still he did not awake. Another hour went by and still he slept, unaware that the sun had been blotted out by a dark indigo curtain that rose swiftly from the northern horizon. Presently, too, this curtain was blotted out by whirling flakes of snow that eddied about the entrance to the cave before dropping silently on the sullen water. And still he slept on, unaware of the silence, a sinister silence broken only by the relentless ticking of the clock on the mantelpiece.

He did not hear the tramp of feet that came cautiously along the catwalk. He neither heard nor saw the door open as Erich von Stalhein, an automatic in his hand, entered the room.

The German counter-espionage officer fitted a cigarette into a long holder, lighted it, and blew a smoke ring into the air. On his face was an expression of extreme contempt. For a little while he considered the sleeping figure thoughtfully; then, reaching forward, he tapped him on the shoulder with the pistol.

Biggles's eyes opened. A shadow of amazement swept through them as they came to rest on the German's austere face. Slowly he raised himself on one elbow.

'You know, von Stalhein, you're becoming a positive pest,' he muttered petulantly. 'Why can't you let a fellow sleep?'

Von Stalhein smiled sardonically. 'Don't worry,' he purred. 'Very soon you shall go to sleep for a long, long time.'

Biggles eyed him reflectively. 'Just what do you mean by that?' he inquired.

'I mean that in the past I have too often delayed what – knowing you – should have been done immediately. On this occasion there is going to be no such delay. I trust my meaning is now plain.'

Biggles nodded. 'Well, I expect as you're a German you can't help it,' he murmured. 'But really, von Stalhein, your mother should have taught you that it isn't customary to shoot prisoners of war. It isn't done. I insist on a fair trial.'

'You had one, on the *Leipzig*.'

Biggles realised the futility of protest. 'Purely as a matter of detail, how did you find your way here?' he asked.

The German held up Biggles's map. 'It was most thoughtful of you to make pencil marks that brought me almost directly to Bergen Ait. An officer of your experience should have known better.'

'You're quite right. I deserve to be shot for such criminal folly,' agreed Biggles. 'How did you get here – in the drifter?'

'Of course. It picked me up, so after landing those saved from the *Leipzig* I came straight on here – not alone, of course. I have a score of marines outside. They are just checking your very interesting stores. I suppose you realise that you have committed a flagrant breach of international law in installing yourself here, on neutral territory?'

Biggles did not enlighten the German as to the facts of the case; he would discover them in due course. 'You're a nice one to talk about breaches of international law,' he sneered.

'Suppose I ask a few questions for a change?' suggested von Stalhein. 'Where are your friends?'

A ray of hope shot through Biggles's mind, for all the time he had been talking, although he had not shown it, one terrible thought was uppermost in his mind. It was Roy, in the signals room, whom he was thinking about, for on his desk lay the most vital document any German agent could hope to secure – the British secret code-book. The German code was there, too, but that didn't matter. At first he had taken it for granted that Roy had been found, and the code-book with him; but now, in view of the German's question, it began to look as if this was not so, otherwise von Stalhein would have commented on it. One of his few weaknesses was vanity, and if he had indeed secured the code-book he could hardly have refrained from gloating over it.

So Biggles merely effected a yawn. 'Why, aren't they here?' he inquired.

Von Stalhein regarded him narrowly. 'No,' he snapped, 'they're not. But doubtless they will return in due course. I'll wait for them – but there is no reason why *you* should. I have a firing party on parade outside. I presume it will not be necessary for me to use force to induce you to report yourself to them. I will make the necessary introduction before the *unteroffizier* takes charge.'

Biggles rose slowly from the bed. 'You won't object to my having a cigarette?' he said politely.

'Of course not,' replied von Stalhein reproachfully. 'Is there anything else I can do for you – any messages – you know the sort of thing? I hate being dramatic, but at such moments as this it is usual—'

Biggles lit a cigarette and flicked the dead match away. 'That's very kind of you, von Stalhein,' he said coldly. 'I hope to do as much for you one day.'

The German smiled confidently. 'Then you will have to be very quick about it. Shall we go?'

Biggles nodded. 'I suppose we may as well.'

Von Stalhein clicked to attention and bowed as Biggles preceded him through the door to the depot.

A squad of marines, under an N.C.O., was in line, waiting.

CHAPTER XV

Happenings on the Rock

Roy was still asleep over his work when the Germans entered the cave, but his door was open, and it must have been some sound made by them that caused him to wake up with a start. For a moment or two, still heavy with sleep, he stared about him uncomprehendingly; then, realising where he was, he looked at his watch, wondering how long he had been asleep.

To his relief he saw that everything was exactly as he had left it. There was nothing to show that Biggles and Algy had returned and visited the signals room, so he assumed, therefore, that they were still away, and he was still puzzling over their prolonged absence when a sound reached his ears that took him quickly to the side window of his cabin, which commanded a view of the entrance to the cave.

The sight that met his eyes caused him to go cold with horror. He blinked, shook his head, and looked again, hoping that what he saw was merely a dream – a very unpleasant dream – for coming along the catwalk was a file of German marines. At the mouth of the cave he could see the boat from which they had landed, and beyond it, a huge fuselage bearing the swastika of the German Air Force. For two or three seconds he could only stare in wide-eyed consternation, his brain racing and his thoughts chaotic; the one fact that he seemed capable of grasping was that in the absence of everybody the base had been attacked in force by the enemy. Not for one moment did he doubt that he was alone in the depot. There was no reason why he should. He assumed automatically that had anyone else been there some sort of resistance would have been made. He was not to know, of course, that the German flying-boat had actually been flown to the base by Algy.

Trembling from shock, he tried to force himself to think clearly, to decide what he ought to do. At first he toyed with the idea of making a rush to the bomb-store and blowing the whole place to pieces, himself with it. Then his eyes fell on the code-books, still lying on his desk, and he knew that his first duty must be at all costs to prevent the British code from falling into German hands. The German code did not matter so much, although it would be better, he thought, if the enemy were kept in ignorance of the fact that it had been captured. Hastily stuffing into his pockets all the loose messages that lay on the desk, he picked up the two code-books and crept round to the rear of the hut – the only way he could go, for the German marines had now reached the depot.

His one idea was to find a place where he could either destroy or conceal the code-books before he was captured, for he could not see how capture was to be avoided. There was only one direction he could take without being seen, and that was towards the rear of the cave, and up the narrow passage he now made his way.

For some time he stumbled on, bruising himself against unseen obstructions, but relieved to discover that the cave went on farther than he expected. Actually, as we know, it extended a good deal farther, but he was, of course, in complete ignorance of what lay ahead.

Not until he had gone some distance and was sure that he could not be seen from the depot did he start to put into operation the plan uppermost in his mind – the destruction of the code-books. Naturally, his instinctive thought was to burn them, and with this object in view he took a box of matches from his pocket and struck one. Hitherto, not possessing a torch, he had been in darkness, so it was in the light of the match that he first saw his surroundings. Somewhat to his surprise, and to his great satisfaction, he saw that the cave, although it had narrowed considerably, continued, so he decided to follow it to the end in a vague hope that the code-books might be saved after all.

For some time, in his anxiety to get as far as possible from the invaders, he struck matches recklessly, but finding his stock getting low he then began to use them more sparingly; all the same, it was not long before he discovered, by counting them, that he had only four matches left, and these he decided to preserve as long as possible. This was, in the circumstances, a natural and wise precaution, but it was to prove his undoing, for in trying to climb over an enormous boulder without using one he lost his balance on the top of it. He made a frantic effort to save himself from falling, even allowing the books to fall from his hands, but the rock was smooth, and his clutching fingers failed to secure a hold. His head came in violent contact with the hard floor on the far side; something seemed to explode in a sheet of purple flame, a flame that faded quickly to blackness as he lost consciousness.

Had he known that Briny and his father, the Flight-Sergeant, were somewhere in front of him, he might have proceeded up the cave with more confidence. In their search for Ginger they had explored the rocks round the mouth of the cave as far as it was possible to go, but finding no sign of him there, they had turned their attention to the other extremity. They both had torches so they were able to make good progress, feeling that at last they were on the right track.

It was Briny who discovered Ginger's broken torch. He was picking his way through the loose rocks of Ginger's fallen cairn when he noticed it, lying half hidden under a boulder. He recognised the type at once, and knew then without any doubt that Ginger was somewhere in front of them.

'I say, Flight, look at this!' he cried, as he picked up the torch. 'He must 'ave come this way.'

'I don't like the look of that,' said the Flight-Sergeant in a worried voice. 'Something pretty serious must have happened or he wouldn't have left his torch behind. The bulb's broken, anyway,' he concluded, sweeping the floor of the cave with his own torch as if he expected to see Ginger lying there.

'He must 'ave gorn up there,' declared Briny, shining his light on the high mass of rock in front of them. 'How did he get up there without a light I wonder?'

'I should say he dropped it from the top,' reasoned the Flight-Sergeant shrewdly.

'But you'd 'a thought he'd 'a come back for it,' protested Briny.

'You would, but evidently he didn't,' observed the practical Flight-Sergeant. 'Give me a leg up; we'd better have a look up here.'

Briny gave him a shoulder, and the Flight-Sergeant gazed speechlessly on the sheet of placid water which he saw in front of him. 'He didn't go this way,' he announced at last.

'Why not?' asked Briny from below.

'Come up and have a look.' Bending down, the Flight-Sergeant caught Briny's hands and dragged him to the top of the rock. 'What d'you make of that?' he muttered.

'Strike ole Riley!' breathed Briny in an awe-stricken whisper. 'He must 'a tumbled in and got drownded.'

'That's how it looks to me,' admitted the Flight-Sergeant despondently. 'I don't think it's any use getting ourselves wet trying to get across. Let's give a hail. Hullo, there!' His voice echoed eerily over the still water.

'He ain't 'ere,' said Briny in a low voice as the echoes rolled away.

'We'd better get back and report,' decided the Flight-Sergeant. 'The C.O. ought to know about this. I reckon he's back by now.'

''Ere – 'old 'ard!' ejaculated Briny suddenly, catching him by the arm. 'Ain't that a light I can see over there?'

The Flight-Sergeant switched off his torch and told Briny to do the same so that they could see more clearly. Together they stared at the grey streak that had attracted Ginger's attention.

'That's daylight all right,' declared the Flight-Sergeant. 'It begins to look as if he may have gone across after all – bearing in mind that he'd lost his torch. I'm going over to have a look at that. You'd better stay here; there's no need for us both to go.'

'That suits me,' admitted Briny. 'I've nearly lorst me 'at twice as it is. You know, this reminds me of a place I once struck with my old shipmate, Charlie—'

'I'll sock you on the jaw and give you something else to remember if you don't shut up remembering things,'

146

snarled the Flight-Sergeant, whose nerves were on edge. He started taking off his clothes and piling them on the rock. 'You stay here till I come back,' he ordered Briny.

''Ow long are you goin' to be away?'

'It depends on what I find over there. If I want you I'll shout.'

'Where do you reckon it leads to?'

'The top of the island, I should say. And I guess that's where we shall find Mr. Hebblethwaite – that is, if he hasn't fallen off. Stand fast.' The Flight-Sergeant slid into the water, and holding the torch above his head, swam on his back towards the streak of reflected light.

–

Ginger was, as we know, on the top of the island. He had been there for some time and was in a bad way.

After seeing Algy's machine disappear round the shoulder of rock he had sat still for some time, thinking that it might reappear and wondering what was the best thing to do. But when the plane did not reappear he set about exploring the place, prompted by the hope that it might be possible to get immediately above the cove and attract attention by shouting.

He soon saw that the top of the island was more or less flat; what slope there was, was towards the place where he stood, which accounted for the seepage of rainwater into the underground lake. Only round the extreme edges was the rock very rough, and here it had been carved into fantastic shapes by the searing wind. There was no herbage of any sort; on all sides the rock lay bare, gaunt, and stark, with the grey edges cutting into the wan autumn sky. The rock, too, was wet from the recent rain, and he found that progress was both slow and difficult. However, after a time he reached the spot he had selected, a place from where he hoped to be able to see the cove, only to discover to his chagrin that it was still out of sight beyond a forbidding *massif* that towered up at the southern extremity of the island.

This mass of rock he eyed with disfavour, for he perceived that to reach the top of it would entail a dangerous climb. Another thing that worried him was the fact that the afternoon was now well advanced, and if darkness caught him still on the *massif* he would find it difficult indeed to get down; and the top of the grim pile was no place to spend the night.

He wondered what the others were doing, and what they were thinking of his long absence. He did not know – and perhaps it is as well that he did not – that Biggles was at that moment on the *Leipzig*, standing before a tribunal, and that Algy was in the cave preparing to take off with a torpedo to sink the liner. When Algy did take off Ginger heard him, but he could not see him, for he had just reached the most difficult part of the *massif*. As the roar of the aero-engine reached his ears he made a hasty descent, hoping to attract the attention of the pilot before the machine was out of sight; but by the time he reached the level part of the island the *Didgeree-du* was a speck in the southern sky – much to his disgust.

Cold and weary, he knew that it would be folly to attempt to rescale the *massif* before darkness fell, so he looked about for the best place to await the machine's return. By the irony of fate, when it did come back it passed within fifty feet of him, but as it was now quite dark it might as well have been a mile away. He wondered who was flying the machine, and what had been its mission, little suspecting that it was Algy returning after torpedoing the *Leipzig*.

Soon afterwards he heard the machine take off again, which was, of course, when Algy set out, with Briny in the back seat, determined to blow up the German store depot. It was, as near as he could guess, two hours later when he again heard the machine returning, and assumed that that would end operations until the following day. To his amazement, within a few minutes he heard the plane go off again, and again he wondered what was going on. This was the occasion when Algy, having flown Briny back to the base, was returning to the sandbank with Biggles's spare kit.

Tired as he was, Ginger did his best to keep awake until the machine returned, for he was not to know that its wheels were stuck fast in the ooze of the sandbank. He was curled up in a fitful sleep between two rocks when the big German flying-boat glided down. Nor did he hear Algy take off again, now in the *Platypus*, on his attempt to bomb the German store depot in accordance with Colonel Raymond's instructions, although the sky was now grey with the dawn of another day. Indeed, he did not awake until the rim of the sun, ominously red, was showing above the eastern horizon.

He was wide awake the instant he opened his eyes, to find that his very bones were stiff with cold. He stamped up and down for some minutes to restore his circulation, and then, with a sort of desperate energy, set about the ascent of the *massif*. Realising only too well that he might not survive another night on the open rock, he took the most fearful chances to reach the top; but at last he got there, and lying flat on his stomach, peered over the edge of the cliff. He was, as he expected, immediately above the cove, but the hail that was ready on his lips remained unuttered. At first he could only stare unbelievingly, trying to force his unwilling brain to accept the awful truth. But there was no getting away from the fact. There, on the cove, near the entrance to the cave, rode a four-engined German flying-boat.

As far as he was concerned it could mean only one thing – the squadron had been discovered by the enemy. And he must be pardoned for thinking that.

For some minutes he lay still, staring down with dismay. Then, with his face pinched from the cold, and his heart heavy, he rose to his feet and started on the return journey to the flat part of the island. Just what he was going to do he did not know, but at the back of his mind there was a wild idea of getting back to the depot by the only way he knew – the way he had come up.

It took him longer than he had expected to get down from the *massif*; and so taken up was he with his task and his melancholy thoughts that he did not notice the change in the weather until a snowflake settled lightly on his face. He stopped abruptly, glaring up at the leaden sky. 'You would pick on this moment to do the dirty on me, wouldn't you?' he grated impotently.

However, he hurried on, but by the time he had reached his immediate objective, the twenty-foot face of rock above the ledge, the snow was whirling round him so thickly that he could hardly see where he was going. At the edge of the cliff he stopped, half bewildered by the flakes that danced before his eyes. Foolishly, he struck at them with his hands in a futile attempt to see the ledge. 'I'm going down if I fall down,' he told himself grimly, as he dropped on his knees preparatory to starting the terrifying descent.

It is likely that he *would* have fallen down, but even as he groped for the first foothold he heard a sound that caused him first to stiffen, and then draw back hurriedly. It was the muffled roar of an aeroplane which seemed to come from somewhere over his head. His lips parted in sympathy for the pilot, whose feelings he could well imagine, for as if the snow were not bad enough, the engine was missing fire on at least one cylinder, in a manner suggesting that a complete breakdown was imminent.

CHAPTER XVI

Strange Meetings

Straining his eyes into the baffling background of snow-flakes, Ginger endeavoured to get a glimpse of the machine, for he could follow its course roughly by the sound. He heard it coming closer, the engine still missing fire, and when it did appear it was so close that he ducked, thinking that it was going to land on top of him. He recognised the machine for one of their own.

It was not difficult to work out what had happened. Either Biggles or Algy had been caught out in a storm, not far from the base, and was now trying to get in. To make the task more hazardous, the engine started to cut out altogether, picking up again in spasmodic bursts, which led Ginger to ascribe the trouble to snow getting into the air intake.

Still watching, he twice saw the vague grey shadow of the machine appear in the semi-opaque pall that hung over the rock, only to disappear again immediately. The second time he actually saw the pilot's head looking down over the side of the cockpit. After that there came a brief lull. The engine was no longer firing, although whether this was due to a complete breakdown, or because the pilot had throttled back, Ginger did not know.

He walked a few paces towards the flat area, and then stood still again, straining his ears for the noise he fully expected to hear – the crash of the machine striking the sea or the side of the island. He was still staring up when suddenly he heard the whine of wind in wires, dangerously close; then, out of the snow, came the grey shape of the machine, straight towards him, its wheels practically touching the rock. Even as he stared aghast, the wheels bumped, and bumped again, but the machine still ran on.

Thereafter he acted purely by instinct, for there was no time for thought. He knew that the pilot had no means of rising again, and that if it went on, in a few seconds the machine would topple over the edge of the cliff. He was already running to save himself from being knocked over with it as this fact flashed into his mind. He might just have got clear, but now he halted, and as the knifelike leading edge of the port wing reached him, he grabbed it and hung on.

He was, of course, instantly carried off his feet, but he had the satisfaction of feeling the machine swing round, and heard the protesting scream of slewing wheels. Then his fingers lost their grip and he fell headlong. The machine rumbled on, slowly, on a new course, its wheel-brakes hissing.

Ginger picked himself up and limped after it painfully, for he had bruised his knee in the fall. By the time he reached the machine Algy was standing up in his seat, goggles raised, looking back over the tail. His face was pale and drawn with strain, but as his eyes fell on Ginger they opened wide.

'Nice work, big boy,' grunted Ginger. 'Have you any chocolate aboard?'

Algy brushed a hand over his face. 'What is this?' he inquired in a dazed sort of voice. 'Where the dickens are we?'

'On top of the island – where else could we be? Didn't you know where you were landing?'

'Landing my foot,' snorted Algy. 'Didn't you hear my motor packing up? What with a dud engine *and* the snow, I should have been glad to get down anywhere – the right side up. I knew I was near the rock because it loomed up at me once or twice, but I thought I was clear of it, gliding down on the sea. Instead of which I suddenly hit the carpet; I had to run on because I couldn't get off again.'

'You nearly fell off it,' declared Ginger. 'If I hadn't grabbed your wing, in another couple of seconds you would have been over the cliff. This isn't Croydon.'

'You're telling me!' Algy climbed stiffly to the ground, bringing with him a bar of chocolate from the pocket in the cockpit. He gave it to Ginger who ate it ravenously.

'I don't get this,' went on Algy. 'What are you doing up here? Why did you stay up here?'

'Because I can't get down.'

'How long have you been here?'

'Since yesterday morning.'

'Great Scott! How did you get here?'

'Through a hole in the rock. But never mind about that. There's a German flying-boat down in the cove. I saw it when I looked over the top this morning.'

Algy laughed. 'That's all right,' he said. 'It's ours.'

'*What!*'

'Biggles and I pinched it last night. Of course, you didn't know about Biggles being a prisoner on the *Leipzig* – von Stalhein got hold of him.' Briefly, he gave the astonished Ginger a resume of events of the past few hours.

'So I went off to lay an egg on the Boche supply depot – which I did; then coming back I ran into this stuff,' he concluded, indicating the snow with a gesture of disgust.

Ginger, in turn, described how he came to be where he was.

'We'd better see about getting down – and the sooner the better,' announced Algy when he had finished. 'We shall have to abandon the machine, for the time being at any rate. Even if we could get the engine right, the weather makes flying out of the question.'

'If you're thinking of trying to fly off the top of this rock, even with the engine right and the weather fine, you'd better forget it. You don't know what it's like. Wait till the snow clears and have a look at it; you may change your mind then.'

'Couldn't it be done?'

Ginger hesitated. 'I suppose it might, at a pinch,' he conceded, 'but it would be a grim business. I should hate to try it, anyway.'

'Then if we can't fly her off we shall have to dismantle her and take her down in pieces,' said Algy optimistically. 'We'd better have a look and see if I damaged her when I bumped.'

They both walked round the wing to the nose of the machine and made a careful examination, but as far as they could see the machine had not been damaged – at least, not enough to prevent her from flying if the engine was put right.

'Smyth will have to come up and attend to the engine,' declared Algy. 'It's our last machine so we can't afford to lose it. Confound this snow! We shall be buried if it goes on. What's the difficulty about getting down?'

'Only a little matter of a twenty-foot drop onto a ledge just about big enough for a seagull to land on. You'd better come and look.' Taking Algy by the arm, Ginger led him to the edge of the cliff. 'That's the ledge we've got to reach,' he said, pointing. 'Do *you* feel like tackling it?'

'Crikey!' ejaculated Algy as he stared down into the void, although the sea was hidden from view by the snow. 'That's not so pretty,' he agreed.

Then, as they both stood staring down, there came a sound from somewhere below them that made them look up and gaze speculatively into each other's eyes. It sounded like a long-drawn-out howl.

'What in the name of goodness was that?' muttered Algy in a puzzled voice.

Ginger moistened his lips. 'There must be some sort of wild beast in the cave,' he whispered. 'Now we *are* sunk. Nothing would induce me to go down there.'

He started violently as a hairy object emerged slowly on to the ledge below. It turned, and a face looked up. It was Flight-Sergeant Smyth. His expression made Algy burst into a yell of laughter.

He recovered himself quickly and addressed the amazed N.C.O. 'What do you think you're doing, fooling about without any clothes on?'

'My togs are just inside the cave, sir,' explained the Flight-Sergeant. 'I had to swim the pond.'

'Pond! What pond?'

Ginger explained about the subterranean lake.

'I see,' went on Algy. Then, to the Flight-Sergeant, 'You've arrived just in time. You'd better go and get your clothes. My machine's up here and I want you to have a look at it.'

'But how is he to get up?' demanded Ginger.

Algy took from the pocket of his flying-jacket the line which he had taken to the sandbank, thinking that he and Biggles might have to enter the shed through the skylight. 'This should help,' he said naively.

'By gosh! What a bit of luck! That will do the trick,' said Ginger. 'Look here! I tell you what. We'll get the Flight-Sergeant up here to look at the engine. Then let me down, and I'll let Biggles know what has happened. I want a change of clothes anyway, and something to eat.'

'Yes, I think it's time you went down,' said Algy seriously, giving Ginger's weary face a searching look. 'I think that's a good idea. I'll stay here till you get back. You might as well bring Briny with you.'

The Flight-Sergeant, with his clothes in a bundle, reappeared on the ledge. He dried himself as well as he could with his cardigan and then got dressed. 'Briny's with me, sir,' he announced. 'He's the other side of the pond.'

Ginger looked at Algy. 'I think we'd better tell him to stay there,' he said. 'I don't see that there's much he can do up here, so he might as well come down with me and give me a hand over the difficult places.'

Algy agreed, and they told the Sergeant to shout to Briny to remain where he was, after which they lowered the rope and hauled Smyth to the top.

Ginger, with the N.C.O.'s torch, was then lowered to the ledge. He shouted to Briny to show a light to guide him, and then made the passage across the lake. The sailor helped him up when he reached the far side.

'Lor' luv a duck, sir, what a time we're 'aving,' Briny greeted him.

'Yes, aren't we?' agreed Ginger without enthusiasm.

'What 'ave you been doin' up here all this time, sir?'

'Mushrooming,' returned Ginger briefly. 'Come on, let's get down. I've had about enough of this hole.'

Without further conversation they assisted each other down the face of the rock where Ginger had lost his torch, and set off down the tunnel, making all the speed they could.

Ginger, who was leading, didn't see Roy until he fell over him. 'Look out!' he cried as he picked himself up. 'Good heavens, it's Roy,' he went on sharply as the light flashed on the pale, bloodstained face.

'Something must 'ave happened, sir,' said Briny in a hushed voice.

'I can see that,' answered Ginger, staring at the two code-books, still lying where they had fallen. 'Yes, by thunder, something certainly has happened,' he breathed.

'It must be pretty bad to have sent him up here with those books,' whispered Briny. 'What could it 'abin, sir?'

'I can't imagine,' replied Ginger, shaking his head, 'unless, of course, the depot's been attacked. I can't think of any other reason that would send him up here with those two books. He must have been trying to save them when he fell off this rock.'

Briny had taken off his jacket, and after getting Roy into a more comfortable position, pillowed it under his head.

Roy showed no signs of recovering consciousness, and there was nothing more that they could do to help him.

'We'd better carry him down, sir,' suggested Briny.

'I doubt if we can manage it – apart from which, I think it would be dangerous,' muttered Ginger. 'He ought to be moved carefully until we see how badly he's hurt. There's a stretcher down below; I'll go and fetch it.' He spoke slowly, for he was wondering what else there might be below. Algy had told him that when he, Algy, had taken off to bomb the German supply depot, he had left Biggles to sleep off his exhaustion. Why had he not come up the cave with Roy if an attack had been made? Again, there had been no shooting; at least, he had heard none, and he felt certain that if shots had been fired he would have heard them. The more he thought about it, the more inexplicable the affair became.

'I'll tell you what we'll do,' he said at last. 'You stay here and look after Roy. If he comes round before I get back, and is able to walk, try to get him down. If not, wait till I return with a stretcher. I'll go on and see what's happened at the depot.'

'Ay, ay, sir.' Briny touched the peak of his ancient cap. 'I remember once seeing a cave—' he began, and then shook his head sadly as Ginger set off quickly down the fissure.

Ginger hurried on, but as he neared the base he slowed down, for he still had an uneasy feeling that something was amiss. Approaching the final opening, he saw that the lights were still on, so he instinctively switched off his torch and adopted scouting tactics.

He heard the Germans before he saw them, and his heart went cold. Peeping round the final obstruction, he knew at once what had happened, for several German marines were standing on the catwalk. Breathless, he could only stand still and watch, wondering what had become of Biggles.

He was still watching when the door of Biggles's room opened and Biggles himself came out. His manner was nonchalant, but behind him walked von Stalhein, an automatic in his hand. There was a gruff word of command. A file of eight marines, armed with rifles, whom Ginger now saw for the first time, marched forward from the back of the mess that had hidden them.

Von Stalhein halted. With military precision he turned to Biggles, clicked his heels and saluted. Then an N.C.O. in charge of the marines stepped forward. He, too, saluted, and said something in a harsh voice.

Biggles nodded. 'Get on with it and get it over,' he said in English.

The words gave Ginger a clue as to what was happening, and for a moment he was nearly overcome by a sense of his own helplessness. But it did not last long. A look of almost savage determination set his lips in a hard line, and he sidled out of the cave to the rear of the signal room. Pausing only for a moment to make sure that he had not been observed, he then slipped cautiously to the canvas-covered pile of stores behind the mess, where, as it was practically dark, he could only grope for what he sought. With a feeling akin to exultation his hands closed over the barrel of a Bren machine-gun, and he drew it out, holding his breath as it clanked against the rock floor. Blessing his foresight, or the lucky chance – he wasn't sure which it was – that had caused him to examine the stores before exploring the passage, he pulled out a box of ammunition and loaded the gun.

Another surreptitious peep round the end of the mess showed him that he had not a moment to lose, for Biggles, smoking a cigarette, was standing with his back to the wall, with the marines in single file in front of him.

Several other Germans were about, but none of them was looking towards the inner extremity of the cave, which in the circumstances was not remarkable; their eyes were on Biggles, so Ginger was able to creep back to the fissure without being seen or his presence even suspected. There, to his joy, he saw that he had the file of marines in line; only the N.C.O., who was standing a little in front of the others, was clear of his enfilade as he brought the gun to bear and squinted down the sights. Von Stalhein was leaning against the door of the mess, a spiral of smoke rising from the long cigarette holder which he held between his fingers.

At a word of command from the *unteroffizier* eight rifles came to the present.

Ginger was trembling with excitement. Without taking his eyes from the sights, or his finger from the trigger, he shouted at the top of his voice, 'Biggles! Run this way!' Then he squeezed the trigger.

Tac-tac-tac... tac-tac-tac... tac-tac-tac... spat the gun, rolling a hideous tattoo in the confined space and filling the air with the acrid reek of cordite smoke.

To Ginger, the rest was a nightmare in which he seemed to be only a detached spectator. He saw Biggles, twisting and turning as he ran, racing towards him, and he saw that there was a danger of hitting him. So he jumped clear of the cave, and stepping aside, stood in the open, holding the dancing gun while he sprayed everything and everybody in sight.

The marines, those who remained on their feet, bolted for cover. Only von Stalhein stood his ground, shouting orders that were not heeded, punctuating them with snap-shots from his automatic in Ginger's direction. A rico-cheting bullet tore a long splinter from the mess door not six inches from his face, and he, too, darted back out of sight.

Biggles reached Ginger and snatched the machine-gun from his hands. 'Steady with your ammunition,' he grated, and began to sweep the depot with short bursts of fire. But answering bullets soon began to splash against the rocks around him, and Ginger caught him by the arm. 'Come on,' he cried shrilly. 'Let's get out of this. This way.'

'Where to?' shouted Biggles.

'I'll show you. Keep going. Everybody is up here.' Ginger darted into the fissure and switched on his torch.

Biggles waited only to send a final burst down the catwalk, and then, still carrying the gun, he followed at Ginger's heels.

'This is a useful place,' he observed calmly. 'Knowing that we've got this gun, it'll take a brave man to follow us up this drainpipe. How far does it go?'

'Right to the top of the rock.'

'Is Roy in here by any chance?'

'Yes.'

'Has he got the code-books?'

'Yes.'

'Thank God for that,' said Biggles earnestly, 'that's all I care about. You know the way. Lead on, Macduff.'

CHAPTER XVII

Reunion

For some time they pushed on as fast as they could go, occasionally stopping to listen for sounds of pursuit; but as none came, Biggles called a halt and demanded to know what had happened, and what was still happening, on the top of the rock. So in as few words as possible Ginger described his own adventures, and explained how Algy, Briny, and the Flight-Sergeant came to be where they were. He then told him about Roy.

'He must have seen the Huns coming, and bolted with the code-books,' declared Biggles. 'I wonder why he didn't warn me.'

'Did he know you were there?'

Biggles clicked his fingers. 'No, now I come to think of it he didn't. He was asleep when I got back. I was asleep, too, when von Stalhein walked in on me. I didn't hear a thing. When I opened my eyes and saw von Stalhein there – well, I'll leave you to guess how I felt. But we'd better get on. With one thing and another we seem to be in as pretty a mess as we were ever in.'

'We could hold this cave indefinitely – against an army,' said Ginger emphatically.

'We could – if we could live on air,' agreed Biggles. 'We'll talk about that when we get to the others. Come on. Apparently von Stalhein thinks he's got us bottled up, so he's not in a hurry to chase us.'

'How many men has he got down there?'

'I don't know.'

'Well, we've got to break through them, or we shall be here for the rest of our lives. Two might get away in Algy's machine, but that's all.'

'You seem to have forgotten standing orders,' said Biggles seriously.

'What do you mean?'

'I mean that our first job, now that we've been discovered, is to destroy the depot. That stuff mustn't fall into German hands. After we've attended to that we'll see about getting away – not before. But I shall have to have a word with Algy before we decide anything definitely. Hullo, here's Roy and Briny.'

They found Roy sitting up, looking shaken, but he smiled when he saw Biggles coming. 'Sorry about this, sir,' he said.

'So am I,' returned Biggles. 'How are you feeling?'

'Pretty fair, sir.'

'Able to walk?'

'I'll have a shot at it, sir.'

'Good. Then let's get up to the top.'

Briny looked surprised. 'To the top, sir?'

'That's what I said. It's no use going down because the place is full of Germans.'

Briny took a pace backward, his face a picture of consternation. 'Blimey!' he whispered.

Ginger led the way up the cave until they reached the buttress of rock that dammed the water in the lake. They helped each other up, and from the top Biggles surveyed the water with a curious expression on his face.

'What do you think of it?' inquired Ginger.

'I think it's going to be very useful,' replied Biggles enigmatically. 'You're wet through already so you might as well come across with me. Briny, you stay here with Roy and keep guard. I'll leave this gun with you. If you hear anyone coming up the cave, let drive. We shall hear you shoot and come back to help you.'

Biggles took off his clothes, and holding up the bundle with one hand, followed Ginger across to the ledge, where they discovered that it had stopped snowing, although the sky still looked very threatening. A hail brought Algy to the edge of the cliff above them. He lowered the line, and in a few minutes they were reunited at the top, where Biggles told Algy what had happened at the depot. 'How's your machine?' he concluded.

'We haven't tested it yet, but it should be all right,' answered Algy. 'The Flight-Sergeant found a piece of solder in the petrol lead; he's taken it out, so if anyone feels like taking off he can have a shot at it.'

Biggles contemplated the prospect without speaking, for it was enough to daunt the stoutest pilot. The maximum run over the smooth part of the rock was not more than a hundred yards; and that was not the worst. At the end of it, fluted columns of weather-worn rock rose vertically some ten or twelve feet in the air, which meant that a machine taking off, failing to get that amount of height, would collide with an obstruction that would smash it to pieces.

'It might just be done,' decided Biggles at last.

Algy nodded. 'That's how I figured it. Who's going?'

'You are.'

'Why me? Why should I get away?'

'I'm not thinking about you particularly; I'm thinking about the German code-book. Von Stalhein doesn't know we've got it, and it's worth its weight in gold to the Admiralty. Whatever happens here that code is going home if it is possible to get it there.'

'I doubt if I've enough juice in the tank to get to England,' said Algy dubiously.

'Is there enough to get you, flying solo, as far as the North Sea?'

'Yes, I should think so.'

'Then that's the way it will have to be. If, when you get to the North Sea, you can't spot one of our ships – well, I'm afraid it's going to be just too bad. But there ought to be plenty of shipping about – destroyers, minesweepers, submarine chasers, to say nothing of merchant convoys.'

'Why don't you go yourself?'

'Because I've got something else to do here. You've got your orders – don't argue.'

'As you say. What are you going to do?'

'First of all I'm going up to the top of that lump of rock and have a look at the cove.' He pointed to the *massif* up which Ginger had climbed. 'By the way,' he continued, 'you took a machine-gun with you last night. Is it still in your machine? If it is I'll take it. With luck I might get a pop at von Stalhein, if he happens to be standing outside the cave.'

'Yes, it's still in my seat.'

Biggles walked up to the machine, and was lifting the gun out when he gave a cry of triumph. 'By jingo! I'd forgotten that!'

'Forgotten what?'

From the rear seat Biggles lifted the time-bomb, which Algy had not used. 'This squib is the answer to a question I've been asking myself for the last half-hour,' he announced enthusiastically.

Algy stared. 'What's the big idea? I'm not clever at riddles.'

'Does your imagination go far enough to give you a picture of what will happen when I blow this charge against the rock that holds all that water in the cave?'

Algy's jaw dropped. 'You're crazy,' he declared. 'It would blow the cave to pieces. In fact, it might blow half the island to pieces. The tunnel would probably cave in and you'd be stuck up here with no way of ever getting down.'

Biggles laughed shortly. 'That's a detail. What is more to the point, a million gallons of water let loose would sweep every man in the depot into the sea – and everything else.'

'But you don't know which way the explosion would expend itself,' put in Ginger aghast. 'You'd bust the dam all right, but you might blow the top clean off the island – or blow the side out of it, causing the whole place to collapse.'

'My orders are to destroy the depot if we have to abandon it,' answered Biggles grimly. 'Whatever else happened, the explosion would release the water, so von Stalhein and his gang would get their ears wet when they weren't expecting it – not that I care two hoots about them. I'm only concerned with flooding the depot before they can shift the stuff out of it.'

'This ought to be worth watching,' murmured Ginger.

Biggles's manner became brisk. 'Algy, put the codebooks in the machine. I'm going up to the top of the rock. If anything unforeseen happens before I get back, take off and head for England. If you have to come down in enemy waters tie something round the British code-book and sink it. Ginger, you come with me.' Putting the machine-gun on his shoulder, Biggles set off up the *massif*.

It was not an easy climb when Ginger had attempted it, but now, with snow about, it was even more difficult. However, by strenuous labour, and by helping each other over the worst places, twenty minutes saw them at the top.

Ginger was the first to reach the edge and look down. He gave an exclamation of dismay.

Biggles joined him. 'That's von Stalhein's drifter down there, in the cove,' he said. 'I knew it was there. That looks like von Stalhein himself standing on the bridge, talking to the captain. I think I'll let him know that we're still alive.' He lay down in the snow, and taking careful aim, poured a stream of bullets down on the drifter.

Von Stalhein made a leap for the companionway and disappeared; some other men who were standing about also darted for cover.

'Rotten shooting,' said Biggles disgustedly. 'I couldn't hold the gun still in this snow; it jumped all over the place as soon as I pressed the trigger.'

A bullet splashed against a rock just below him, and whistled away into the leaden sky.

Biggles drew back. 'There's no sense in making targets of ourselves,' he said. 'They won't show themselves again for a bit. I've seen all I wanted to know, anyway, so we may as well get back.'

Ginger caught his arm and pointed seaward. 'What's this coming?' he cried.

Biggles looked up. 'A couple of German destroyers, I fancy,' he said evenly. 'Von Stalhein must have called them up by wireless. It doesn't make much difference; I don't see how we could have got out, anyway. We couldn't get near that flying-boat without coming under fire of the drifter. Let's hope the destroyers come into the cove.'

'Why?'

'You'll see. I think you'd better stay here while I go down and get the bomb in position. I'll ask Algy to wait until it goes off; then, if he gets back safely, he can tell Raymond what happened. You watch the destroyers. If they come into the cove, let me know by raising your arms above your head. I shall take that as the signal to blow the charge. Is that clear?'

'Clear as daylight.'

'Good. I'll get down now. After the bang you'll be able to watch what happens.' Biggles smiled and hurried down to where Algy was waiting by the machine. His manner was still inconsequential, but his heart was heavy, for he knew that the last hour of the base had come, and he felt that he ought to have made better use of it. He knew, too, that except for something like a miracle, their own time had come. Whether they were blown up by the bomb, or whether they went down through the cave to surrender themselves to von Stalhein, it would come to the same thing in the end. Not that he contemplated going down. His orders were to destroy the base and he was thankful that he had a means at hand to achieve that object. He had always had a feeling that the end might come this way, for it was as obvious to him, as it had been to Colonel Raymond, that such a base, situated as it was practically in enemy country, could not last for any great length of time.

'What's happening in the cove?' asked Algy as Biggles joined him.

'It seems to be getting busy. There's a drifter and a German flying-boat already there, and two German destroyers just coming in,' smiled Biggles. 'Our friend von Stalhein might almost be justified in thinking that he has got us all safely bottled up at last.'

'Have you any reason to suppose that he hasn't?'

'None whatever. Well, that's all. I want you to stand fast and wait for the result of the explosion before you take off. You will then be able – I hope – to tell Raymond that we wrecked the base before the Boche could shift the stuff. You'd better not start your engine yet. Von Stalhein has no idea that we've got a machine up here, and we don't want him to know, or the destroyers might start slinging shells across before you can get off.'

Algy's face was expressionless as he held out his hand. 'Cheerio,' he said. 'I shall fly back here, of course, if I get the code-books home. If I can persuade the Air Ministry to let me have one I'll borrow a flying-boat; so hang on, if you can, on the off-chance.'

Biggles smiled as he squeezed Algy's hand. 'Do your best, old lad,' he said. Then, turning to the Flight-Sergeant, 'Bring the line and help me down to the ledge,' he ordered.

Whistling softly, he picked up the time-bomb and walked towards the cliff.

CHAPTER XVIII

Biggles Strikes Back

Flight-Sergeant Smyth lowered Biggles to the ledge and waited for further instructions.

'Drop the rope,' Biggles told him. 'I shall need it. Thanks. Now listen carefully. You can see Mr. Hebblethwaite from where you are I think?'

'Yes, sir.'

'Very well. There are two German destroyers on their way here. If they come into the cove Mr. Hebblethwaite will signal by raising both hands above his head. You will pass the information on to me via Briny, whom I shall send across to this ledge. I shall send Roy on over here too. I shall be at the far side of the lake.'

'Very good, sir.'

Biggles undressed, coiled the rope about his middle, and picking up the bomb, shouted to Briny to show a light. Arriving at the far side, he was pleased to find Roy looking much better, and sent him across to the ledge. He then ordered Briny to lower him to the bottom of the rock that dammed the water, where he waited until the message had been passed on to him that Ginger had made the signal. He was relieved to get it, for more than once stealthy sounds coming from below suggested that the enemy were scouting up the fissure.

He timed the bomb for a quarter of an hour, and placing it in position, piled around it all the loose rock that he could find. He then ordered Briny to pull him up, and together they crossed over to the ledge, from where, after the rope had been thrown up, they were all hauled to the top.

Biggles ordered everyone farther away from the cliff in case the explosion should start a landslide, and then looked about him. Ginger was still on the top of the *massif*, looking down into the cove. Algy was standing by his machine ready to start up at an instant's notice. The others were standing near him.

'How long before the balloon goes up?' shouted Algy.

'I set the bomb for a quarter of an hour, so there are still about ten minutes to go. I'm going up to the top to join Ginger. Don't be in a hurry to take off. If anything unforeseen occurs, get off right away without waiting for me to come down; otherwise hang on, and I'll try to give you some definite information to take to Raymond.'

Algy nodded. 'Good enough. But don't wait too long. I don't like the look of the weather; it may start snowing again.'

Biggles glanced at the sky. 'It doesn't look too good,' he admitted, and then set off up the *massif*.

He was still only halfway up when there was a muffled roar, and the whole island quivered like a jelly. He was nearly thrown off his feet, and for the next minute or two was kept busy dodging rocks that had been shaken loose and were rolling down the steep side of the *massif*.

Ginger, lying at the edge of the cliff, watching the destroyers manoeuvre into position in the cove before dropping anchor, clutched at the rocks on either side of him as his perch shook under the violence of the explosion. Several pieces of rock on the face of the cliff were shaken loose and went hurtling down into the cove; some fell sheer, others struck the cliff again lower down and bounced far out over the water. Shouts of alarm rose from below; men appeared on the deck of the drifter, von Stalhein among them; others appeared at the mouth of the cave. Some were launching a dinghy.

After that there was a brief lull, although pieces of rock continued to detach themselves from the side of the cliff and whirl downwards, sometimes taking minor avalanches of loose shale with them. Then, from the very heart of the rock, it seemed, came a terrifying rumble, like distant thunder. The rock began to tremble anew, and Ginger experienced a feeling of acute alarm not far short of fear, for the sensation was one of lying on a volcano about to burst into eruption. His alarm was in no way lessened when a great mass of cliff broke away, and with a roar like an express train went plunging down into the void.

By this time the destroyers, their propellers threshing the water into foam, were turning towards the open sea. On their decks men were running about in a panic. The drifter followed; being smaller it moved faster, and trying to cut across the bows of one of the destroyers, came into collision with it. There was more shouting.

Ginger turned and saw Biggles coming hand over hand up the *massif*. 'Look out!' he cried shrilly. 'The whole island's falling to pieces!'

The words had hardly left his lips when the cliff in one place started to bulge; it was as if it were made of elastic, and was being forced out under terrific pressure. Then, with a crash like thunder, the bulge burst. A mighty torrent of water shot clear into space. Rocks and water went plunging down together. Simultaneously, from the mouth of the cave there issued a swirling yellow flood.

Ginger felt Biggles throw himself down beside him, but he neither looked at him nor spoke. He was too spellbound by what was happening below. At first the falling rock and water prevented a clear view, but as the first pent-up energy of the water subsided somewhat – although a cataract continued to pour down the cliff – the scene became clearer.

It was a terrifying spectacle that met his eyes, more like an upheaval of nature than an artificial catastrophe. Before the weight of water, the three vessels were being swept about like toy ships. One of the destroyers had rammed the drifter amidships and had stuck fast. Both were grinding against the spit that formed one arm of the cove. The second destroyer, with black smoke belching from its funnels, still had its nose pointing towards the cliff, but in spite of its engines, was being slowly carried backward, and was in danger of colliding with the other two vessels. The flying-boat, being lighter, had already been swept out to sea, and now drifted helplessly.

The flood still pouring from the cave went swirling out to sea, a turgid yellow tide that carried with it all sorts of debris, and made a clear line of demarcation with the deep water. Men were clinging to the wreckage which, Ginger noticed, consisted largely of broken timbers, obviously the remains of the buildings of the depot.

'What a picture,' muttered Biggles in a tense whisper. 'I wish I had my camera. Raymond will never be able to say we didn't go out with a bang. What's happened to the cliff underneath us?' He strained forward trying to see it.

'Mind you don't go over!'

Biggles backed hastily. 'There seems to be a tidy hole there. I hope this piece we're on doesn't collapse; it doesn't look any too safe. Hullo, look at the drifter; she's sinking. The crew are abandoning it judging by the way they're jumping on to the destroyer. There goes von Stalhein. That fellow seems to bear a charmed life.'

'He probably thinks that about you.'

Biggles grinned. 'True enough,' he agreed. 'The other destroyer's going to get away, now that things are a bit quieter.'

'It looks like it. Still, she doesn't look any too happy. I bet her wireless is buzzing, asking for help. They'll have to hang around to pick up the people who are marooned on the rocks.'

Several marines, presumably survivors of the party that had been in the cave, had managed to secure a foothold on the rocks that ringed the cove.

'Well, what happens next?' inquired Ginger, watching the second destroyer back slowly out to sea.

'Ask me something easier. We've done about all we can do. Even if we could get down through the cave, which I doubt, I don't think we could take on a destroyer single-handed.'

'We could stop anybody from getting up here.'

'Yes, I think we could do that, but why need they bother to come up? They know we can't get away. All they have to do is sit where they are and wait for us to fall off from want of food. We've one card up our sleeve though. They don't know we've got a machine up here, so it'll shake them when Algy takes off. I may as well tell him to go; there's no point in him staying here any longer now that the fireworks are over.'

One of the destroyer's guns flashed. A shell whined up and sprayed the rock with shrapnel.

'Who says the fireworks are over?' muttered Ginger drily. 'They can see us evidently. We'd better get down.'

Biggles turned towards where Algy was standing; cupping his hands round his mouth he let out a hail. 'All clear!' he shouted, pointing to the sky. 'Tell Raymond we've flooded the place and bust up a destroyer and a drifter at the same time.'

Algy waved to show that he understood. 'Cheerio!' he yelled, 'I'll be back in a couple of days.'

Biggles caught Ginger's eye and smiled. 'Trust old Algy not to be left out of the finale. All the same, I don't see what he can do if he does come back – but it's no use telling him not to.' He sat down on a rock to watch the machine take off.

Ginger squatted beside him. 'I shall be glad when he's up topsides,' he said anxiously. 'I am by no means sure that he's got enough room to get off. If he touches those spikes of rock with his wheels—'

'Don't think about such things,' protested Biggles.

Algy was now in his seat. The propeller came to life.

'I hope there isn't another piece of solder in that petrol pipe,' murmured Ginger.

'He's testing her now,' put in Biggles, as the noise of the engine rose to a crescendo, and then died away again as it was throttled back.

'It doesn't sound too good to me,' declared Ginger, with his head on one side.

'She's giving her revs, anyway, or he wouldn't be so crazy as to try to take off,' returned Biggles. 'There he goes.'

The *Platypus* was racing across the flat part of the rock, apparently to certain destruction. Fifty yards from the jagged teeth that barred its path the wheels had not lifted.

'He's deliberately holding her down,' said Biggles, whose face was deathly white.

Twenty yards from the edge of the cliff the *Platypus* jerked into the air, its wheels missing the rocks with a foot to spare.

Ginger wiped imaginary perspiration from his brow. 'Phew,' he gasped, 'I can't stand much of that. I—' He broke off suddenly and started to his feet.

Biggles, too, sprang up, his lips in a straight line. Comment was unnecessary. The engine was spluttering. There came the explosion of a backfire. The engine picked up again, but only for a moment. Another splutter, and it cut out dead.

As soon as the engine had started missing, the nose of the machine had tilted down. Now it went into a glide, and began a flat turn back towards the rock, about a hundred yards behind it.

'He'll never do it,' said Biggles in a dull voice. 'He can't get back. It's impossible. He'll go nose first into the cliff if he tries.'

What he had said was obviously so true that Ginger did not answer. He was incapable of speech. With his muscles as taut as if he were flying the machine himself, he could only watch. He saw the machine turn away from the island as Algy, too, realised that he was attempting the impossible. A moment later the *Platypus* disappeared from sight below the level of the cliff.

'He's going down on the sea – it's all he can do,' snapped Biggles, and started off down towards the place where the machine had disappeared, jumping from rock to rock in a manner that was little short of suicidal. The Flight-Sergeant, Briny, and Roy were also racing towards the place. With his heart in his mouth, Ginger followed Biggles.

Breathless, they arrived at the edge of the cliff just as the snow began to fall again, although it was not yet too thick to prevent them from seeing the machine land heavily on the water. But the captain of the destroyer had also realised what was happening, and now the long grey hull, flinging a bow wave high into the air, came racing towards the helpless aircraft.

'I'm afraid it's all over bar the shouting,' said Biggles heavily. 'He hasn't a chance.'

'He seems to be mighty busy doing something,' observed Ginger, staring at Algy, who was now standing up in his cockpit. 'What's he doing?'

'I know what he's doing,' said Biggles bitterly. 'He's tearing the British code-book to pieces so that he can set fire to them.'

'What! In the machine! He'll have the whole thing in flames in a couple of minutes. If his tank catches fire he'll blow himself up.'

'He'll risk that as long as he destroys the book,' declared Biggles. 'Confound the snow,' he added viciously, as the blizzard suddenly thickened and blotted out the sea. They could not even see the water.

For a minute the watchers on the cliff stood still, listening, vainly straining their eyes.

'I thought I heard a shout,' muttered Ginger.

The words had hardly left his lips when a violent explosion again shook the rock, although the noise was muffled somewhat by the snow. A moment later came the sound of debris falling into the water.

'That's his tank gone up.' Ginger's voice was little more than a whisper.

Biggles said nothing. With his chin cupped in the palm of his hand he sat staring, white-faced, into the driving snow.

CHAPTER XIX

Marooned on the Rock

For some time nobody spoke. The only sound was the chugging of an invisible motorboat somewhere on the sea below.

At last Ginger tapped Biggles on the shoulder. 'Come on,' he said. 'There's no sense in sitting here getting smothered with snow. If we don't soon get back to the cave we may not be able to find it.'

Biggles got up. 'I was trying to work out a way of getting that code-book back, but it's got me stumped,' he said despondently. 'However, as you remark, it's no use sitting up here in the snow, unable to see a blessed thing; we may as well have a look at the cave – if it's still there. If it isn't – well, it'll be interesting to see how they propose to get us off this rock. They won't just sail off and leave us here, that's certain.'

'The only thing they could do would be to shoot us up from the air with machine-guns.'

Biggles reached for their own gun. 'Two can play at that game,' he said grimly. 'Poor old Algy; if only he could have got away with those books I shouldn't have minded so much what happened here. Ah well! I suppose it was bound to come to this sooner or later. Let's get back to the cave.'

They all made their way through the drifting snow to the edge of the cliff.

'The ledge is still there, anyway,' observed Biggles, looking over the top as he tied the rope round his waist. 'Let me down first.'

With the gun in his hands he was lowered to the ledge. The others followed, Ginger, who came last, scrambling down at the end of a running line, with the rope looped round a projecting piece of rock at the top of the cliff.

Entering the cave, they saw at once that the lake was no longer there. Where the water had been yawned a wide black crater, but the passage across it offered no great difficulty. At the far side they found that the rock that had dammed the water had been shattered by the explosion; beyond it, the fissure was almost choked with debris, and Biggles looked at it dubiously before he advanced.

'Take it quietly everybody, or we may have the whole place down on our heads,' he warned the others.

Moving with extreme caution, taking care not to disturb loose rocks, they went on, noting the results of the escaping flood.

It was Ginger who saw the new exit first. Biggles had just pulled up with a cry of warning – or it may have been dismay – for they had reached a place where the fissure was almost completely blocked with pieces of loose rock, jammed together by the colossal weight of the water. All their torches were on, and it was no doubt due to this that the grey light which entered the cave from the left at first passed unnoticed. Ginger, happening to look that way, let out a shout. 'Here, what's this?' he cried. 'It looks like a hole. It must be the place where the water burst through the side of the cliff.'

As quickly as they dared they made their way to the spot, and soon saw that what Ginger had surmised was indeed the case. A large portion of the side of the cliff had been forced out by the sudden weight of the released water, leaving an enormous cavity into which the snow now drifted.

Biggles made his way cautiously to the edge and looked down. 'I can just see the cove,' he announced. 'I should say it's about eighty feet below us.'

'Is there anybody about?' inquired Ginger.

'I can't see anybody.'

'Then they must be back in the cave, trying to get up to us.'

'I don't think they'll get past that mass of rock – the place where we were held up.'

'If they can't get up, it also means that we can't get down.'

'I'm by no means anxious to get down just yet, anyway,' said Biggles slowly. 'I think the snow is getting thinner. Let's sit here for a bit until it clears. We'd better see what's happening below before we do anything else.'

Resting the gun against a boulder, Biggles sat down to wait. Ginger squatted beside him, and the others leaned against the rock. As Biggles had remarked, the snowstorm was passing, and presently it was possible to see most of the cove.

'Where the dickens has everybody gone?' muttered Ginger, scanning the scene below in search of the Germans whom he fully expected to see there.

'Don't ask me,' replied Biggles. 'I can only think that the second destroyer must have picked them up.'

'But it was making for Algy's machine. Surely it wouldn't have tried to get back into the cove through all that snow. Visibility must have been zero.'

'There's the destroyer, and the drifter, at any rate,' observed Biggles, as visibility improved and it became possible to see the two vessels, still locked together against the spit. The destroyer had sunk by the stern, with her bows still in the drifter's hull. Both appeared to be deserted.

'This has got me whacked,' went on Biggles, with a puzzled expression on his face. 'Where the dickens have the crews gone?'

'The lifeboats aren't there,' the Flight-Sergeant pointed out. 'They must have taken to the boats when the destroyer started to founder.'

'But where could they go? Why can't we see them? You'd have thought they'd have come ashore.'

Briny stepped forward. 'Excuse me, sir, I didn't like to mention it before, but when you was a'sittin' on the top there, just after Mr. Lacey flopped down in the ditch, I thought I 'eard a motorboat. I've got a pretty good ear for engines, and I said to myself, I said, if that ain't the blooming motorboat wot let me down, then I never 'eard it.'

Biggles stared, trying to grasp the significance of what Briny had said.

'Just a minute,' put in Ginger sharply, turning to Biggles. 'Didn't you say that the drifter had picked up the motorboat? If so, it might have brought it here.'

'That's right,' conceded Biggles.

'Then they might have cleared off in the motorboat – or taken the lifeboats in tow.'

'Even so, that doesn't explain why they should suddenly rush off, knowing that we were on the island.'

'They may have gone to the other destroyer.'

'Yes, but where *is* the other destroyer?' cried Biggles, indicating the open sea, for the snow had now practically stopped, and it was possible to see for two or three miles.

'Great Scott! Look! There's Algy's machine,' shouted Ginger suddenly.

Biggles stared as if he could not believe his eyes; but there was no possibility of mistake. The *Platypus* had drifted into sight, close to the rocks below them. It seemed to be in an undamaged condition, but of Algy there was no sign.

'He must be in the water – unless he managed to get ashore,' ventured Roy.

'Hark!' said Biggles suddenly.

Over the water came a hail. 'Ahoy there!'

'What the dickens! That wasn't Algy's voice,' swore Biggles.

'It certainly wasn't,' agreed Ginger emphatically.

Then to their ears came the muffled beat of an engine, and they all stared at the shoulder of rock from beyond which the sound seemed to come. And as they stared, moving very slowly, a long, sleek body came into sight, just above the surface of the water.

'Look out! It's a U-boat,' snapped Biggles, grabbing the gun. Then he stopped, staring incredulously as the rest of the steel deck came into sight. On the deck was a gun, and behind it stood a crew of British bluejackets. Nobody spoke as the conning-tower came into view, and then Ginger let out a yell, for standing talking to two British officers was Algy. The submarine forged on, its white ensign fluttering.

'Ahoy there!' yelled Ginger, nearly going over the cliff in his excitement.

They saw Algy look up and point, and in a moment a dozen faces were staring at the hole in the rock.

'Talk about fairy godmothers, they aren't in it,' declared Biggles, a flush on his pale face. 'Where have you sprung from?' he shouted.

'We've come for that code-book!' shouted the submarine commander.

Biggles remembered his signal to Colonel Raymond and understood what had happened. The Admiralty had sent for the valuable document. 'Watch out!' he roared. 'There's a Boche destroyer about somewhere.'

'It won't worry us,' answered the naval officer. 'It's—' He jabbed his thumb downwards.

'That must have been the bang we heard,' said Ginger. 'It wasn't Algy's tank; it was a mouldy hitting the destroyer.'

'Come down – I've got to get back. I daren't hang about here!' shouted the submarine commander. 'Where are the people off that other destroyer?'

'They must have seen you and pushed off in their lifeboats. They had a motorboat with them.'

'I see. Come on down.'

'Stand fast. We're not sure that we can get down.'

Biggles made his way quickly to the cave, but it did not take him long to ascertain that any idea of getting down that way was out of the question. How far the blockage extended it was impossible to say. At some risk he dragged a few small pieces of rock aside, only to reveal more rock, apart from which he nearly brought the roof down on his head. 'It would take weeks to clear a way through here,' he told Ginger, who had followed him.

'But that means that we can't get down at all.'

'It begins to look like that,' admitted Biggles. 'Maddening, isn't it, with the submarine so close.'

'Perhaps they can get a line up to us?' suggested Ginger. 'We'll ask them.'

They hurried back to the opening and informed the naval officer of the position. 'Can you get a line up to us?' concluded Biggles.

The submarine commander conferred with his officers. 'No!' he shouted up. 'We haven't a line long enough. Even if we had we couldn't get it up to you.'

'That means we're stuck here,' declared Biggles, looking round the horizon which, now that the snow had cleared, could be seen. His eyes fell on a line of lifeboats heading southward, and the mystery of the abandoned ships was explained. He realised that von Stalhein must have seen the destroyer torpedoed, and had promptly fled in the motorboat. Biggles's roving eyes picked out something else, a smudge of smoke far beyond the boats. 'What's this coming!' he shouted, pointing towards it.

The submarine commander studied the distant hull with his binoculars. 'It's a German cruiser,' he announced. 'If you're coming with me you'll have to buck up. I daren't risk my ship by staying here.'

Biggles thought desperately, but he could find no way out of their quandary. 'All right skipper,' he shouted at last, 'you get off and take the code-books. We shall have to take our luck.'

'Sorry – but you can see how it is.'

Biggles waved good-bye.

Suddenly Algy cried, 'Can you get back to the top?'

'Yes,' Biggles told him, whereupon Algy spoke rapidly to the naval officer, at the same time pointing towards the

German flying-boat, which was still drifting about half a mile away. Then he looked up.

'Get back to the top of the rock,' he bellowed. 'You'll have to buck up.'

'I don't know what he's thinking of doing, but we'd better do as he says,' declared Biggles. 'It's no use staying here, anyway.'

A parting wave and they were on their way back to the summit of the island. Panting with exertion, they made their way across the empty reservoir to the ledge, and then, by means of the rope, to the top.

'I've got it,' said Ginger, as they ran across to a position from which they could look down on the submarine. 'He's going to fetch the flying-boat.'

'But he can't land a boat up here,' protested Biggles, as they reached their immediate objective and scanned the sea for the submarine. But it had gone. The German cruiser was still coming at full speed, and was now not more than five or six miles away. The *Platypus* was a smouldering wreck, burnt to water-level. The big flying-boat was racing over the sea towards the island.

'He must have set fire to the *Platypus* to prevent it from falling into the enemy's hands, so he must be pretty confident of getting away,' declared Biggles.

A moment later the aircraft left the water and roared up towards the top of the rock. Five pairs of eyes watched it anxiously as it climbed rather higher than the island, and then swept round with the obvious intention of flying straight over them. As it passed over the level area a bulky object fell from it and plunged downward. Another followed, and another. There was no time for more, for by this time the machine had overshot the island; but it banked steeply and retraced its course. Two more objects detached themselves to bounce on the rock.

'I've got it!' yelled Biggles. 'They're brollies.'

Ginger stared aghast. 'Does he think we're going to jump off the top of this place?' he gasped.

'That's it. There's no other way.' Biggles ran forward to retrieve the parachutes, the others following him.

By the time they had each picked one up the flying-boat had cut its engines and was gliding down. It landed, and taxied nearly – but not quite – under the overhanging ledge, which, fortunately, happened to be on the side farthest from the cruiser.

Algy's voice floated up. 'Come on!' he shouted. 'I'll pick you up. Get a move on. It's that or nothing.'

'Where's the submarine?' called Biggles.

'Gone.'

'Has it got the code-books?'

'Yes.'

Biggles gave a sigh of relief and started getting into his harness. Ginger and the Flight-Sergeant were doing the same thing. Afterwards they helped Briny and Roy, neither of whom had ever made a parachute jump.

Biggles looked down, and judged the distance to be a little over four hundred feet. 'We shall have to pull the ring as we jump,' he announced. 'Jump out as far as possible to get clear of the rocks.'

Briny's face was ashen. 'You don't mean to say, sir, that I've got to go over there?' he whispered plaintively.

'That's just what I do mean,' answered Biggles firmly.

'I daren't do it, sir, s'welp me, I daren't.'

'Be a man, Briny. Think what a tale you'll have to tell when you get home. Think of how you'll be able to start your stories: "I remember the day I jumped off the top of Bergen Ait—'"

Briny's eyes opened wide. 'Why, yes, that's right, sir,' he gulped.

'And I'll tell you something else,' declared Biggles. 'When we get back I'll let you tell a yarn right through without interrupting you.'

'You will, sir?'

'Honest. Only buck up about it. If you hang about much longer you'll find yourself landing down the funnel of that perishing cruiser.'

Briny advanced to the edge of the cliff. He looked down and shuddered. 'It's no use, sir,' he moaned. 'I daren't—'

'Over you go or I'll throw you over,' snarled Biggles, pretending to fly into a fury. 'Don't forget to pull the ring!' he screamed as Briny tottered into space.

Ginger put his hands over his eyes. He couldn't bear to watch. He held his breath, waiting for the splash.

'Phew! He's all right,' said Biggles, drawing a deep breath. 'The brolley's open, so he can't take any harm now. Algy will attend to him. Your turn next, Roy. Don't forget to slip your release gear as soon as you touch the water.'

'Very good, sir.' Roy stepped forward, and waited until Algy had dragged the dripping Briny into the flying-boat. Then he jumped clear.

His father gasped his relief as the parachute mushroomed out.

'You go next, Flight-Sergeant,' ordered Biggles.

The N.C.O. jumped without a word.

'You'd better wait a minute before you go, to give Algy time to pick them up,' Biggles told Ginger.

Ginger grimaced. He had made many jumps, but never one like this. However, he clutched the rip-ring with his right hand and launched himself into the void, head first, in the professional manner.

A shell screamed over the island; it burst in the air, spraying the rock with shrapnel.

Biggles ignored it. He jumped out as far as he could, and slipped the quick-release gear the instant his legs dragged in the water. Slipping off the harness, he swam to the door of the flying-boat just as Algy was dragging Ginger in.

'Get a move on,' he told Algy. 'That cruiser's coming up fast. Keep low for a bit when you take off, then she won't be able to see us on account of the island being in the way.' He pulled himself on board and sank into the spare pilot's seat, wiping the water from his face. 'Lucky thing those chaps carried brollies,' he told Algy seriously.

'Lucky thing I remembered seeing them, too,' snorted Algy. 'You might give me credit for something once in a while.'

'Good work, old lad,' agreed Biggles, 'but we'll talk about that when we get home. Just see about getting us there.' He turned to Briny, and noticed that there was something different about him, although he could not make out what it was. His expression was disconsolate. 'What are you looking so miserable about?' he inquired.

'I've lorst me 'at at last,' answered Briny in a broken voice. 'It fell orf as I was comin' down. You don't know what that 'at's been through, sir. I remember once—'

He stopped as if from force of habit.

Biggles nodded encouragement. 'Go on,' he prompted. 'What did you and your old shipmate Charlie do?'

'Well, would you believe that,' muttered Briny, scratching his head in confusion.

'Believe what?'

'I've forgotten what I was going to say.'

His confession was greeted with a yell of laughter.

'Tough luck, Briny,' said Biggles sympathetically. Then he turned back to Algy. 'You'll have to watch your step when we get over the North Sea,' he warned him. 'Don't forget that we're carrying swastikas and black crosses, and there must be a whole crowd of our fellows fairly pining to get their sights on one.'

'That's all right,' replied Algy. 'When I left the submarine Sparks was tapping out a signal warning all ships and aircraft not to shoot at a four-engined Dornier flying-boat flying at a thousand feet. If Roy will get to the wireless cabin and get into touch with the Air Ministry, no doubt they'll tell us where to land.'

'That was well thought out,' declared Biggles. 'Good enough! Let's get home.'

The four engines of the flying-boat burst into song, and she streaked away from the secret base that was a secret no longer.

CHAPTER XX

Home

Forty-eight hours later, after landing at an R.A.F. Marine Base on the East Coast, Biggles, Algy, and Ginger reported to Colonel Raymond at the Air Ministry. They found him waiting for them.

Biggles, who was in rather low spirits at what he regarded as his failure to keep the secret base going, was more than a little surprised at the reception they received. It was certainly not what he had expected. Instead of criticism he found only satisfaction amounting to jubilation.

Colonel Raymond waved aside Biggles's apologies for losing the base and his machines. 'My dear fellow, that code-book was worth a hundred machines to us, apart from which you certainly made things hum for a little while. The work you have done more than repays us for what we spent on the base – in fact, you managed to do a lot more than we expected.' He smiled. 'Did any of you get any sleep at all?'

'Not much,' admitted Biggles. 'But I don't see that we did an awful lot—'

'Rubbish. What did you expect to do – destroy the entire German Navy and Air Force? If any one unit achieves greater success than yours I shall be very much surprised. Directly or indirectly, you were responsible for the destruction of an ammunition dump and a marine store depot; you interrupted lines of communication which has held up the movement of German forces from Poland to the Western Front; you have sunk a submarine, a drifter, and a liner that was to have been used for troop transport in the Baltic. Two destroyers have been sunk, and you have captured one of the enemy's latest marine aircraft. On top of that you get hold of the latest naval code – all without a single casualty and for the loss of only four aeroplanes which can easily be replaced. You certainly didn't waste any time.'

'But we've lost the secret base.'

Colonel Raymond smiled knowingly. '*A* secret base – yes; but not the only one we possess. We've been busy in the Baltic for some time past. Bergen Ait isn't the only island that threatens Germany. But that's for your private ear – perhaps I shouldn't have told you. We sent you to Bergen Ait – I'll be quite frank with you – because it was nearest to the German coast, and consequently the most dangerous – for the enemy as well as you. D'you know how long the Higher Command estimated the base would last after you took it over, before it was located by the enemy?'

'Six months?'

'Twenty-four hours at most.'

'You didn't tell me that,' murmured Biggles reproachfully.

'Naturally – we didn't want to discourage you,' Colonel Raymond informed him coolly. 'But work it out yourself. You were in enemy waters, with hostile craft all round you, both on the sea and in the air… No, Bigglesworth, it couldn't last more than a few days at the very outside.

When you went out of this door I never expected to see you again.'

'We're difficult people to kill,' murmured Biggles, winking at Ginger.

'Evidently. Well, that's all. Believe me, we're grateful for what you've done, and no doubt your work will be mentioned in dispatches when it becomes safe to do so. At the moment we prefer to keep quiet about it. Now take yourselves off and let me have a full report in writing on what happened at Bergen Ait; after that you can take a few days' leave – but don't go too far away.'

'Why not?'

'Because – well, you see, we may need you again.'

Biggles nodded. 'I had an idea you might,' he said slowly as he walked towards the door. 'Good-bye, sir.'

The Colonel smiled. 'Perhaps it would be better to say *au revoir*,' he suggested softly.